DAN

After the Finfer

First Edition
ISBN: 978-0-9897607-2-0

Art on cover: Christine Shan Shan Hou, 2013
lazy river
6.75 x 10 inches
collage on paper

Design and composition by Danielle Dutton
Printed on permanent, durable, acid-free recycled paper
in the United States of America

Dorothy, a publishing project
PO Box 300433
St. Louis, MO 63130

dorothyproject.com

DAN

JOANNA RUOCCO

MELBA ZUZZO stood in the yard chewing tiredly on several pieces of gum. The day had barely started, and, as soon as it was over, another day was bound to begin. When would it end?

If only there weren't leap years, thought Melba. Every 365 days, the calendar would lose several hours and, by now, there wouldn't be any days left at all.

Melba strapped a helmet to her head. Beneath her feet, the yard felt compacted, dead herbage dried into a pleasant thatch. The unvented helmet was lined with a squishy foam that served no purpose unless she brought her head into some kind of contact. She stood, helmeted, preparing to launch herself forward.

For a moment, she was held in position, perhaps by the air.

Nearly six quadrillion tons in all, thought Melba. As she recalled this fact, she felt the weight of it. She considered lying down. But was it wise? Melba's mother had once warned her against lying down out of doors in foam.

"Pam Dempsey!" her mother had cried. It was summer and a downpour had cleared the pollen from the air. Melba and her mother had gone for an uncharacteristic walk together through the center of Dan, enjoying the freshness. They sat on a propane tank in the sunlight, passing a baggy of mulberries back and forth over the tank's bright red cap.

"Pudgy Pam!" Melba's mother shook her head admonishingly. "Pam the ham! Pam Dempsey." Melba's mother mashed the baggy of mulberries in her fist. "Poor Pam! She wandered away from the Halloween parade in her lobster suit and never returned. 'I'm just going to nap in the woods, Gigi,' she said. A harmless nap in the woods. I thought nothing of it. Pam Dempsey," sighed Melba's mother. "She put up quite a struggle, but all she could do in that floppy foam suit was flip herself over, supine, prone, supine, prone, or push herself around in circles with her feet, that's what the authorities said when they saw the patterns in the disrupted leaves. The body was gone, of course, dragged away by coydogs."

The foothills around the village of Dan were densely wooded, and it was true that at night the dells echoed with the mating songs of coydogs. Despite these congruencies, Melba had found it difficult to accept certain details of her mother's story. Her mother never understood Pam Dempsey, thought Melba. Gigi Zuzzo was always striving! She was always running about, eating pralines and searching for lost keys, making vigorous checkmarks on secret lists she stowed in her purse or executing a series of invisible but excruciating isometric exercises. Her mother could not understand why a girl might abandon a parade to lie quietly in a bed of leaves.

Melba imagined hundreds of discombobulated children, their faces garishly painted, bouncing around in plastic jumpers, their mouths crammed with Swedish Fish, a few of them tooting hand-held noisemaking devices, others hurling gourds. She imagined Pam Dempsey slipping away from the throngs, walking slowly into the forest, and lying down in the leaves. As night fell, she would have felt peaceful and warm in her lobster suit, blinking up at the forest canopy, watching as frost blanched the humid branches of the maple trees.

Melba imagined the pleasant pressures exerted on Pam Dempsey's limbs by the mouths of many coydogs, their teeth battened by the foam of a lobster suit. Pam would have kept very still. She would have let herself be pulled into the foothills by coydogs, and then beyond the foothills into another town, or even all the way to the sea.

"Pam Dempsey!" said Melba now in the yard. The dense air absorbed the sound in an instant.

Sometimes Melba wondered if Dan was under some sort of quarantine. It seemed more difficult to come and go from Dan than could be accounted for by simply the mud and the ice and the mountains with their crevasses and deadfall snares. But who could have quarantined Dan? The federal government was rumored to have such powers, but the federal government seemed extremely remote, and Melba had heard that the federal government did not even exist in a state—as did Dan, and Henderson, another town Melba's mother mentioned from time to time—but rather occupied a nebulous zone, almost but not quite its own country.

All at once, the elasticity of Melba's gum exhausted itself. She spat a hard blue bean into the darkness of early morning. At the edge of the yard, the swarming thicket of black currant bushes and slime-fluxing hemlocks had grown thicker in the night. Melba approached, cautiously, arms extended. She pinched a currant between her fingers and sniffed. She found the smell distinctive, like the feces of a fisher cat. Earlier, Melba had found traces of such feces tracked through her house. But perhaps those had not been the feces of a fisher cat? Perhaps the small stains were so many trampled currants?

There is no use scrutinizing stains, thought Melba. At least with the naked eye. Their compositions are so complex.

With some difficulty Melba pushed into the thicket and extracted her bicycle from its caul of humus. As she pedaled through Dan she fixed her eyes on the dim grid of rooftops that dropped down the slope of the mountain toward the leachfield. It was an election year, and many of the rooftops sported slogans, even the mansard of the European, Helmut Pirm. Melba steered her bicycle into the large drain that ran beneath Lops Street, the warm water spraying up, rinsing the mud from the chain and the hubs.

Melba noticed a large bird running beside her, wings slightly outspread so that Melba had to assume they created significant drag,

8

enough drag to strain the legs of the bird, which were doubtlessly strained already by the bird's swift pace as it ran beside her, gaining on her, through the drain. Melba pedaled faster and exited the drain well in advance of the bird. She felt flushed and triumphant and rang her bell several times, laughing. Mark Rand, Melba's landlord, lived on Satin Street, and Melba rang her bell again as she passed his house. Melba didn't mind Mark Rand. He was short and personable, and even though he had attached earlobes, he seemed trustworthy to Melba. Still, she wished he wouldn't store his agricultural chemicals in the shed behind her house. Shortly after she'd moved into the house on Hotot Street, she surprised Mark Rand pushing a hand-truck of damaged vats across the yard. Melba stood with her coffee watching him struggle over the thick ferns and the scat-like piles of oak galls.

"Hello, Mr. Rand," said Melba and Mark Rand grunted at her over the hand-truck.

"Hello," grunted Mark Rand. Then he paused, letting the base of the hand-truck rest on a coil of old garden hose so that he could address her more fully. "I am joyful, Melba," said Mark Rand. "There is nothing sweeter to the eyes of a landlord than the sight of his tenant taking her ease on the well-maintained back stairs of a high-quality rental unit, her hand cozying a mug of hot beverage. Moments like these remind me why I remain committed to property management, instead of devoting myself full time to the more lucrative business of antiques." He gestured to the vats on the hand-truck, which were,

Melba noticed, extremely old. "I could auction these," continued Mark Rand. "And for quite a bit of money, too, but it wouldn't feel right. I want you to enjoy them, Melba."

"Thank you, Mr. Rand," said Melba.

"Don't touch them," said Mark Rand. "But know that your shed is filled with priceless antiques. Take pride in them."

Of course the vats were antiques, thought Melba. Mark Rand's agricultural chemicals must have been left over from the days when the town of Dan was a pleasing patchwork of family farms criss-crossed by sportive sheep and grains of golden pollen. Such a Dan scarcely seemed possible.

"Dan wasn't always a quagmire, was it?" Melba asked Mark Rand impulsively.

"No, Melba, it was not," said Mark Rand.

"What happened?" asked Melba, but Mark Rand didn't answer.

His hand-truck had been partially swallowed by a sinkhole and its excavation required his full attention.

Sometimes Melba wondered if she would ever discover the reason behind Dan's transformation. Here and there, she'd encountered signs of Dan's former prosperity: a quarry with tractor attachments rearing from the murky waters, a ticket stub from a county fair. But the residents of Dan could recall very little about the history of the town.

"You're not exactly a spring chicken," Helen Drake had said reprovingly, when Melba asked her about the Dan County Fair. "Why should I remember? What about you Melba?"

"Me?" said Melba. Surely she wasn't as old as Helen Drake! But maybe she was. It was hard to tell with ages. But if Melba Zuzzo was as old as Helen Drake, she would certainly remember the Dan County Fair! Melba had been led to believe that hers was a particularly good mind, sharp and retentive. In grammar school, Melba had been the favorite of the principal, Principal Benjamin. It made sense that a principal would take to an intelligent child, an insightful child, a child of wit and aptitude, but perhaps Principal Benjamin was a different kind of principal. Perhaps he did not favor bright children. Perhaps he had been drawn to Melba precisely because he had sensed in her an utter lack of distinction, a pinched, lackluster quality that would only intensify with the years, eventually yielding a person so small and blanched he could put her in the pocket of his mustard-colored frock coat, marking her absently from time to time with his thumbnail as he might mark a nutmeat. There were principals with such proclivities, Melba thought. Who could say one way or the other about Principal Benjamin? Principal Benjamin had disappeared long ago.

In the basement of the school, the police found the tattered corner of a mauve bandana, monogrammed with Principal Benjamin's initials and redolent of vinegar and paste.

"I'm sorry, Melba," said Officer Greg when Melba arrived at the Dan Police Station. "I know you were close to Principal Benjamin, but there is nothing you can do to help."

He brought Melba into the booking room.

"Unless of course you understand *that*," said Officer Greg, pointing to the enormous poster on the wall.

"The periodic table," said Melba.

"Well it's not an eye chart!" said Officer Greg. Then, at the look on Melba's face, he gentled.

"Whatever happened to Principal Benjamin, it was an act of nature," said Officer Greg. "Not a crime. We're calling in an expert to consult—," Officer Greg jerked his thumb at the periodic table, "*that*. Many would argue we're over-stepping our bounds pursuing the case at all."

Officer Greg sighed. "I can't explain any more," he said. "It's confidential police business. But maybe you can help us, Melba. How would you describe Principal Benjamin's handwriting?"

Melba thought long and hard.

"Like blood droppings from a flea," said Melba, "if the flea walked in straight lines across the page instead of bouncing from place to place."

Officer Greg took a ziploc bag from his pocket and held it close to his face. Melba could see a white rectangle through the dingy plastic.

"Yup," said Officer Greg. "It's a match. Thank you, Melba. That will be all."

Officer Greg didn't allow Melba inside the Dan Police Station again. Weeks later, when the expert had delivered his full report on the isotopic compositions of noble gases and the case was officially closed, *The Dan Banner* ran an article lauding Officer Greg for his policemanship. The article made no mention of Melba Zuzzo's role in the investigation. Melba Zuzzo read it a dozen times, as though savoring her misuse.

"Misused," said Melba Zuzzo, and her voice rang out prophetically in a way that she did not enjoy.

Another possibility, Melba admitted, and a strong possibility at that, was cognitive degradation. She may indeed have been an intelligent child. Her inability to remember things might be a recent condition, a sign that her mental faculties had been compromised by her proximity to Mark Rand's agricultural chemicals. Lately Melba had noticed certain changes. She was more agitated and her weight fluctuated, six pounds or more, between nightfall and morning. Melba was a tertiary feeder, and the chemicals had already affected the bottom of the food change. When Melba found vermin in her house—chipmunks and the occasional beaver—she could tell that they were not developed properly. They had weakened teeth and forepaws. Melba couldn't help but laugh at the chipmunks as they tried to grip the Brazil nuts she piled in the nut well of the party platter. Their jerking movements reminded her of the time she tried to work the claw vending machine at the movie theater. The claw lurched all around, but the apertures between its prongs were too vast to give it purchase on the tiny, densely stuffed heads of the ostriches and giraffes that wallowed in the depths of the acrylic cabinet. After a few moments, the claw froze open and retracted, and no matter how many times Melba struck the sides of the machine with her fists, it only dangled on its short chain, twitching feebly.

"The Dan Movie Theater!" scoffed Helen Drake when Melba explained the movements of the chipmunks. "You see Melba, you are old!"

Maybe the trouble was adulthood and not agricultural chemicals, thought Melba. She had been a precocious child, but could one be a precocious adult?

Now in the gray sky above the rooftops of Dan, the sun was rising, overlarge and irregularly shaped, ramified by the refractive moisture droplets that made the air in Dan so suffocating to breathe. Melba's exultation relaxed into a drab tranquility. Catching sight of her face in a shop window, she confirmed that her gratifying race with the bird had not suffused her cheeks with the becoming glow gratification brought to the cheeks of most others. The blood had come up in splotches.

She stopped her bicycle to peer at herself more closely in the window. She felt a burning in her left earlobe and stroked the earlobe grimly. Against her finger, the earlobe felt hard and weepy. It troubled Melba to consider her earlobe "weepy," as though the sense organs, in this case, the eyes and the ears, could share their functions. The very notion brought to mind the lower-order animals, how they ate and defecated through a single hole. Such a simplification of the bodily processes would not appeal to the men and women of Dan. They took so much pleasure in the buttery crumpets and extra-soft pretzels Melba sold by the dozen in the bakery, and they reacted so negatively when, in casual conversation, Melba linked the crumpets and pretzels, however loosely, to any kind of output: vomit, excrement, or esophageal refluxus. Melba shuddered to imagine what the townsfolk would say if they needed to contend with the effects of reverse evolution. Most likely, though, they were simply unaware. Melba had never heard even a whisper about reverse evolution in her science classes, and not around town either. One time, Melba remembered, people had milled around in talkative groups right in the center of Dan, eating pretzels and discussing issues, but the conversation had focused on technological innovation.

"Fold-out couches are a disgrace," shouted one woman. "They're gimmicky, not worthy of their patent. Does anything good come from beneath the cushions of couch? Disease! Fossilized nachos! And we spend money adopting polar bears!" the woman's voice shook with emotion, but the others did not take up her topic. It was widely known that the woman's teenage son was a bounder given to serial, ungrateful tenancies on the couches of others, and that her comments did not represent the impartial assessment of technology that the tenor of the discussion demanded.

"What about mops?" a man thundered, leaping up onto the balustrade of the gazebo. "They're just bits of rags tied to a stick! The totemic peoples exchanged such items with their neighbors to prevent sexual intercourse within the family clan. But do mops really serve such purposes today?"

Before Melba could catch the answer, Mayor Bunt arrived to announce that the tar-and-chips road maintenance activity had ended for the day.

"The roads are open," announced Mayor Bunt and the people dispersed, Melba included. She had hoped to find the man who spoke so warmly about mops. His passionate intensity set him apart from the other men she had known, but at the same time, something about his short arms and humped back struck her as oddly familiar. She shoved through the crowd but by the time she reached the gazebo he was gone. That was years ago and, having never seen him again, Melba was forced to conclude that he was a salesman of sorts, just passing through Dan on his way to a hub of commerce.

Melba was about to push off again on her bicycle, when a man flung open a second floor window in the house across the street. He waved at Melba.

"Bev," the man cried, "Bev Hat." Melba squinted at the man, who was now leaning out the window gripping a bottle of hydrogen peroxide.

Melba knew Bev Hat. They'd been schoolchildren together back when Bev Hat was Bev Horn. Bev Horn had always showed promise and eventually she had blossomed into Bev Hat, a popular young mother. The last time Melba had seen Bev Hat, she was scrubbing stroganoff from a Turkish rug and singing in a high, clear voice. She was vigorous and thin, with the kind of grueling beauty that Melba's mother found so impressive. Everyone was impressed with Bev Hat!

Even Randal Hans, back when he was Melba's boyfriend, seemed to think admiring thoughts about Bev Hat.

"Is it fair to say that Bev Hat's beauty is like new fallen snow?" he asked Melba. "Or does that make her seem cold?"

"Are you writing a letter to Bev Hat?" Melba asked, surprised by her shrilling tone. Randal pushed back his chair and put his pencil behind his ear.

"I was only thinking aloud, Melba," he explained. "Sometimes I take notes when I think aloud." He picked up his coffee mug and his stationary and went outside to sit on the back steps. After a while, he came back inside for more coffee and he and Melba found themselves in a spirited conversation about the life cycles of fruit flies. Melba never felt happier than she did in those days, drinking coffee with Randal Hans.

"Your coffee is something else, Melba," Randal Hans said. "It's special." Melba had told him the ingredients—water, coffee grounds, puffed wheat, honey—but not the proportions.

"I don't know how they puff wheat," Melba admitted.

"You don't?" Randal Hans replied. "I'm surprised." Randal Hans always claimed to think a lot of Melba's intelligence.

"Would you like more honey?" asked Melba.

"I have a theory," Randal spoke with a serious look on his face. "People claim that the lentil was man's first food, but I think that food was honey."

Randal Hans rarely offered opinions and Melba felt happy that she had incurred one of his ideas. She had never shared this fact with him, but her life had been significantly improved by honey. Due to her ingestion of honey, up to a half pound a day, she had developed immunity to the histamines in the local flora.

When Melba was a child, she was plagued by chronic congestion and as a result she had developed polyps in her sinus cavities.

Her sinus cavities, Dr. Buck had explained, were abnormally dank and deep, with almost no airflow, the perfect conditions for anaereobic life forms, such as polyps, to proliferate. Dr. Buck's office frightened Melba, with its photographic murals of circus clowns and the complicated many-bladed instruments soaking in the utility sink.

"Have you been to Kentucky?" asked Dr. Buck, opening the speculum in Melba's nostril somewhat wider than she would have preferred. Her eyes began to tear and she struggled cautiously with her lower body, pulling up her knees and delivering short kicks. Dr. Buck inserted a penlight in her nostril.

"There is wonderful spelunking in Kentucky," said Dr. Buck, "and certain of the caves have properties, properties you would not believe if they were described to you by someone less respected than a family doctor, someone slightly cracked. Can you think of anyone, Melba?"

Melba thought of the redheaded people in Dan. There were many redheaded people in Dan and Melba's father, Zeno Zuzzo, always said they were different from normal people. Then Melba thought of Hal Conard, who traveled all around the county because he shoed horses.

"Hal Conard?" guessed Melba. Dr. Buck extracted the speculum and penlight and tossed them in the sink. He dropped heavily onto a rolling chair and drew the chair rapidly forward with his feet. He stood and lifted Melba off the examination table, settling back into the chair, with Melba on his lap. He wiped away her tears with his gloved fingers. The wet latex on Melba's skin made squeaks.

"Do you have an eye otter?" joked Dr. Buck, tenderly.

"I hope not," said Melba and Dr. Buck sobered. He squeezed Melba close.

"Hal Conard is exactly right," said Dr. Buck. "You wouldn't believe Hal Conard if he told you about a cave in Kentucky with special properties. Hal Conard shoes horses, but have you ever seen a horse in Dan? I didn't think so. In fact, Melba, answer me this: have you ever seen a horse?"

"Yes," said Melba.

"Think carefully before you answer," said Dr. Buck. "Because there are certain canids—those are dogs, Melba—that can be shaved and groomed to resemble other animals, raccoons, lions, even horses. Can you be absolutely certain that what you saw was a horse and not one of these canids?"

Melba thought carefully. She could not be absolutely certain.

"Of course, you can't be certain," said Dr. Buck. "Without the opinion of an expert there's no such thing as certainty. Now what if

Dr. Buck tells you that you've never seen a horse? That, in fact, there are no horses?"

Melba tried to pull away from him but he held her in his squishy embrace. His heart was beating against her shoulder.

"But what about the ponies?" Melba asked. "The ones on the islands?"

"Islands," repeated Dr. Buck darkly.

"Aren't there islands?" asked Melba. She had seen drawings in the display cases at Dan Elementary, each of a brown hump rising from jagged blue crayon marks, a curving tree with five skinny leaves rising from the center of the hump. The humps were islands. There were so many drawings and they were all the same! How could the children all draw the same thing if it wasn't real? There had to be islands.

"There are islands," said Melba. Dr. Buck said nothing. Moving his feet, he crept the chair across the floor to the window. He reached out and pulled on the window shade so it flapped up and Melba could see the window glass, flecked here and there with white deposits.

"There is Dan," said Dr. Buck, and Melba tried to look through the glass. She had always known that she lived in Dan, but she had never thought about what Dan was made of. Melba looked intently at Dan.

She could see her father sitting on the hood of Dr. Buck's car holding an olive and an extremely large knife. She could see, behind her father, the outlines of Dan Elementary on the hill and the children climbing on the midget submarine and Kubelwagon, and, behind Dan Elementary, she could see the steep muddy foothills that rose steeply into the steeper muddy mountain range, the closest peak accessible only by funicular device.

Dan.

Dr. Buck laid his gloved fingertips lightly on the back of Melba's neck. She felt his breath tickling the exposed line of skin away from which she folded the left and right halves of her hair.

"What do you see?" asked Dr. Buck. Melba was holding her breath and she had to exhale noisily before she could speak. Dr. Buck patted her back.

"My father," said Melba Zuzzo.

"Melba, I am your father," whispered Dr. Buck. Melba stiffened. She cried out. She slapped her palms instinctively against the window as though trying to reach Zeno Zuzzo, who had shaved a sliver of olive and was contemplating the sliver where it clung to the blade of the knife. Dr. Buck began to laugh.

"Not biologically, Melba," he laughed. "But we are just alike in our souls, don't you think? Do you like pralines?" He gripped Melba under the armpits and set her on the ground, then rose to fumble in a kidney-shaped tray. He extracted a praline.

"I like pralines," he said. "But I would rather you have it. This praline is for you." Melba took the praline between her lips, then pushed it with her tongue so that it fit between her gums and her cheek.

"You didn't eat the praline," said Dr. Buck.

Melba nodded. "I did," she said, the saliva puddling around the praline so that a sugary tendril of drool escaped from the corner of her mouth.

"You did not," said Dr. Buck, sadly. "No matter. I will write you a prescription."

That very night, Melba developed a system of nasal irrigation, snorting a broth of white pepper, tobacco leaves, and mustard powder. Within the week, her polyps had dissolved. Adopting a maintenance therapy of rigorous honey consumption, Melba attained a fully oxygenated, even ruddy good health. As the years passed, she experienced small ignominies—thinning hair and frequent infestations of eye mites—but she did not seek out Dr. Buck. He asked about her, Melba knew this, and sometimes he came into the bakery, pretending not to recognize her, but leaving little gifts: paper bags of empty gel-caps for her to fill with whatever she wished.

Melba wondered if she would ever find out for sure about horses and islands. If she would need some sort of reference material or travel regimen.

The man in the window was still calling to her.

"Bev," he called. "Bev."

Seeing another human being operating so vehemently under a false perception made Melba feel a kind of relief. She smiled and waved at the man in the window, walking her bicycle forward with her legs on either side of the top tube.

"It's not Bev. It's Melba," called Melba. "From the bakery."

The man in the window gave a jerk, striking his head against the window sash.

"Oh Bev! Why have you come back as Melba?" the man moaned.

"Oh Bev! Why Melba? Why Melba?"

Melba could no longer bear to crane her neck at the man. She let her helmeted head fall forward, slumping over her handlebars.

The man was still shouting. "Why Melba? Why Melba?"

"Why, Melba," came a voice close at hand. "Now you've done it."

Melba dragged her head to the upright position and saw Hal Drake, the successful machinist. He patrolled the streets of Dan in the early hours when Officer Greg was still asleep. Melba had never seen such a somber look on his face.

"That's Ned Hat up there, Melba," said Hal Drake, grimly.

"Ned Hat?" Melba's eyes flew to the figure in the window. "But that's an old bald man! Ned is different. He isn't like . . ." Melba faltered.

"Like what?" Hal gave a short, harsh laugh. "Like me, Melba?"

"Like *that*," said Melba. "I mean, like that man in the window."

"He is now," said Hal. As he spoke, he worked his mouth as though he were chewing on the sides of his tongue. Melba looked away.

"A lot can happen to a man in the night," said Hal, quietly. "You wouldn't understand."

"He's frothing at the mouth!" cried Melba.

"Let him be," said Hal. "It's the peroxide."

"Someone has to do something," protested Melba. She glanced uneasily up and down the empty street. "Where's Bev?"

Hal went rigid.

"She's dead, Melba," said Hal. "She died yesterday."

Melba squeezed the grips of her handlebars. She inclined her chin to look again at the man in the window and she felt the weight of her helmet tug her head backwards.

Melba's thoughts of Pam Dempsey returned to her. Melba wondered if it was still possible to walk off, to lie quietly. Her head lolled.

"It was helium poisoning," continued Hal. "She was filling campaign balloons for Mayor Bunt . . ." his voice broke.

"Ned thinks I'm Bev Hat!" burst out Melba, straightening her neck with a sudden rush of isometrics.

"Ned doesn't know what to think," said Hal. "It's very early in the morning and he hasn't gotten much sleep. He'd have to be crazy to imagine that Bev has come back as you, Melba. Where would you have gone, then, answer me that? If you're Bev, where's Melba? It would be better if he'd never seen you, but now that he has, there's nothing you can do. He'll forget this whole thing soon enough. The best thing you can do is get to work. I'll handle Ned Hat."

"Bev!" Ned yelled.

"Go Melba!" said Hal, and he slapped the back wheel of Melba's bicycle as he aimed a flare gun at Ned Hat's window with his free hand. Melba pushed off and pedaled faster than she ever had, flying down the hill, until she saw the lighted windows of the bakery shining onto the dough dumpster that Bert Bus, the garbage man, had forgotten to drag back into the alley where it belonged by day, upright amid the liverworts.

The lights in the bakery were always on because the owner, Leslie Duck, thought the lights gave the impression of industry.

"Folks see the lights," Leslie Duck had said, "and they say to themselves: 'even now, even in the dead of night, the bakers are working in the bakery, baking fresh and golden pretzels,' rather like elves, Melba."

Melba was a docile employee, but something—the reference to elves—forced her to question Leslie Duck.

"I've often wondered," she said, "can't elves see in the dark? Like opossums? Couldn't they work the mixers in the dark?"

Leslie Duck stared at Melba for a moment.

"Well, that sounds a little sinister, Melba," he said finally. "That sounds strange and sinister. You don't go around town saying things like that, do you Melba?"

"Of course not," said Melba quickly. "I don't talk about work. It's impolite, what with so many people unemployed. Imagine if I started saying that opossums worked in the bakery when half the young men in Dan are so idle and bored they've petitioned scientists to put them in chemical comas! There would be a riot. The bakery would be burned to the ground."

Leslie Duck did not look convinced, but Melba began to apply rock salt to the pretzels with such avidity that eventually he nodded with satisfaction and left her to her task.

Now Melba ran about the bakery, uncovering trays of pretzels and crumpets and sliding them under the display case. She realized that her skirts were damp with dirty water from the storm drain and that her hair had been flattened and burred by the helmet. She tied an apron over her muddied shirtfront and dropped onto a stool behind the counter. She tried to forget about Bev Hat. Bev Hat was just one woman and her absence around town could not be as significant as, for example, the absence of a whole group of women. Melba recognized that even the absence of a group of women was not, strictly speaking, *significant*, that is, from a statistical perspective. The population of Dan was not large, yet somehow it was difficult to account for all of the residents.

Melba's mother had once offered Melba an explanation.

"That Ann Dump!" Melba's mother had cried. Ann Dump was the town clerk, and not a good one. Under Ann Dump's clerkship, many vital records in the town hall vault had been consumed by snails.

"That Ann Dump!" said Melba's mother. "She encourages snails. Have you ever noticed the cucumber slices in the town hall? Every surface is covered with cucumber slices! That Ann Dump is feeding the snails! She's lured every snail for miles around into the town hall with her cucumber slices."

Melba had looked around her mother's kitchen. For years, snails had been wearing runnels in the floorboards, and in these runnels, Melba could see several dozen snails in transit. She identified at least three varieties of snail, including the Eastern Melampus, the snail for whom her younger sister, Melampus, had been named. Melba felt the urge to pick a snail from the wall. Surely, with one of these evidentiary beings in her hands, Melba could at last contradict her mother. How could Gigi Zuzzo claim that Ann Dump's cucumber slices attracted every snail for miles around when the Zuzzo household was filled with snails, every day more snails than the day before? The town hall was very close to the Zuzzo's, just across the gully, on Flop Street. Even for snails, the trip couldn't take long. But maybe it hadn't occurred to them yet? Gigi Zuzzo was a forward thinker. Her ideas were certainly more advanced than the ideas of snails. The pace of a snail exodus was bound to be slow, so slow that the signs could very easily be missed.

Melba had hesitated, fingers hovering above the snail on the wall. What if she failed to contradict her mother, and instead only managed to provoke her? Gigi Zuzzo often said that Melba was a provoking daughter, quarrelsome, with habits befitting an earlier kind of person, a person from pre-history. In pointing out her mother's incorrect assessment of Ann Dump's cucumbers, Melba did not want to prove her mother correct in her assessment of Melba. Melba jerked her fingers away from the snail, but all at once the extensor muscles in her arm contracted. Her arm straightened and she slammed her palm against the wall. The wet pop made Melba grimace.

Why couldn't Melba master fine motor skills? Maybe she was like a pre-historical person. Melba imagined a pre-historical person. The pre-historical person was squatting in carnivorous ferns, using a rock to smash a mosquito against her own face. A modern person would deal with the mosquito differently. A modern person would react with dexterity and cunning, fabricating a short switch from the carnivorous ferns and flicking it against her face, concussing the mosquito while leaving the bridge of her nose and the facial skin intact. How had the pre-historical person developed into a modern person, a person with this capacity for mental sequencing and gestural precision? Through what course of study?

In high school, Melba had taken both history and phrenology, but neither class had included a unit on pre-historical people. Mr. Sack, the history and phrenology teacher, did not believe in textbooks. Instead, he distributed modeling clay, which the students used to shape the noses of 19th century naval heroes. Melba enjoyed shaping noses, but she hoped for exposure to something more. She grew listless, each nose she produced more snoutish than one before, until finally she decided to visit Mr. Sack in his office after school.

"Knock, knock," said Melba, and the door swung open. For a moment, it looked and sounded to Melba like something large had just bounded behind Mr. Sack's ficus tree, and Melba couldn't help but conclude that Mr. Sack was secretly blind and keeping a guide animal hidden in his office. She began to back away from the door, but suddenly Mr. Sack was at her side, ushering her roughly to a low footstool.

"Welcome to my solitary idyll, Melba Zuzzo," said Mr. Sack with a broad smile. Melba looked away shyly, pretending to inspect his tall bookshelf. On every shelf, blocks of modeling clay had been carefully grouped according to color, whites with the whites, grays with the gray, taupes with the taupe.

"If you'd like to borrow a block, I have a sign-out sheet," said Mr. Sack, still smiling. His thighs were close to Melba, and from her seat on the footstool, she could inspect them at eye-level. The wales on his corduroy trousers had been worn down, exposing the thin, sheer fabric beneath, the greasy silver color of a well-thumbed spoon. Mr. Sack selected a taupe block from the shelf, but Melba declined the proffered block and clipboard with a shake of her head.

"Oh, no thank you," said Melba. She gazed about wonderingly. She had missed school offices, with their lovely potted trees and heavy, dented furniture and wall-calendars and clocks! Since Principal Benjamin had disappeared, she had never imagined she'd enter one ever again, but there she was, in an office in the late afternoon, when the other young people were mingling with each other in the muddy clear-cut beneath the funicular device. Melba was never the type to mingle with young people, and though she wasn't yet exactly mingling with Mr. Sack, she began to enjoy his proximity. Mr. Sack's office had a sour and talcy odor, which increased her enjoyment. The odor reminded Melba of the family bathroom after one of her father's diluvial showers, the white puddles he left after he'd rinsed his hair with vinegar and patted his body dry with an assortment of unperfumed powders. Melba sighed as Mr. Sack settled himself in his chair and looked down at her, legs crossed. After a moment, he spoke.

"You may rest your head on my knee," he said, and Melba started.

"Oh, that's very kind," she said, and then, realizing that her attempt at polite refusal had surrendered at polite, she remained perfectly still as Mr. Sack took a small velvet pillow from his desk drawer and positioned it on his lap.

"I so often rest my head on things, though," said Melba. "Warm, unfrosted cakes. Freshly piled laundry. I'd better not." She giggled nervously but Mr. Sack only shrugged.

"The vertical carriage of the human head is marvelous," he said, "as are the orthognathic jaws and mobile tongue, but it often results in hypertonicity of the neck muscles. "

"Why don't we ever talk about the neck muscles?" asked Melba. "Or about the tongue? There's so much I want to know."

Mr. Sack took a nose from the desk drawer and regarded it sadly, his index fingers thrust deep in the snoutish nostrils.

"Melba," said Mr. Sack, finally. "You've grown tired of noses. Hush! Don't argue! I'm a teacher and I understand things. You think I should widen the scope of my classes. Well, you're wrong, Melba.

Dangerously wrong. The students in this school have excitable passions. Sometimes they kiss each other feverishly in the halls, or stand up in class, screaming, 'I am thy vessel! Fill me, dark prince, with the power of evil!' Certainly, you've noticed."

Mr. Sack shook his index fingers so that the nose dropped to his desk with a dull clunk.

"The students in this school can't handle the stimulus of absolute knowledge. They need routine and fentanyl lozenges."

Melba felt a deep thrill at this unexpected confidence and she leaned forward eagerly.

"I'm not like the other students, Mr. Sack," said Melba. "My airflow is too restricted for kissing and I hate to make a scene." She lowered her voice. "Mr. Sack," she confessed, "Principal Benjamin told me about epochs. He said I would learn about them someday. I thought he meant in high school, but maybe he meant at some other point in life, when I'm in the workforce, or taking a course at a retirement community. Mr. Sack, I have a problem," whispered Melba, almost breathless, "I just can't figure out what time is made of." Mr. Sack worked a mauve lollipop out of his pants pocket and he offered it to Melba without speaking. She ignored it.

"Mr. Sack," whispered Melba. "Sometimes I think time must be like a kind of jelly. A jelly that makes us move slower than we would otherwise, because isn't time just a way of delaying the inevitable? If there wasn't time, everything would be over. But then I'm afraid I'm wrong. I'm afraid that, if there wasn't time, everything wouldn't have started yet, and we'd be at the beginning. Then I feel so daunted I can barely move. That's why I fall down sometimes in class and lie in the aisle. Tell me, Mr. Sack," said Melba, eyes glowing. "Is time a jelly? A clear jelly, like nothing we've ever eaten? Principal Benjamin was going to explain it to me, but then . . ." Her voice broke and she slapped a hand over her mouth, horrified at her uncharacteristic display of excitement. Mr. Sack had pressed the back of his hand against his forehead, as if to ward off her words, and his body trembled. He tore the wrapping from an elongated lollipop and jammed it into his mouth, cracking the hard glossy cone with his teeth.

"You won't get an answer out of me, Melba," said Mr. Sack. "You say you're not like the other students, but how can I trust you? Any one of them would say the same thing. Principal Benjamin trusted you and you know what happened to him."

Melba felt as though her body had spun a few degrees around her vertebral column. She leapt to her feet, steadying herself against Mr. Sack's desk.

"What happened?" she demanded. "What happened to Principal Benjamin?"

Mr. Sack's eyelids were drooping. His chin bobbed against his shirtfront.

"Mr. Sack," said Melba. "You can trust me, Mr. Sack."

Mr. Sack's voice was so thin Melba could barely make out the words.

"Miasma," rasped Mr. Sack.

"Miasma?" repeated Melba.

"Not jelly," rasped Mr. Sack. "Miasma. Time."

"Oh!" cried Melba, but before she could form another thought, Mr. Sack slid down his chair onto the floor. He dragged his torso beneath the desk and drew in his legs. Melba stood in the empty-looking office. She'd felt like she was the only person on the earth and retreated quickly into the hall.

There in her mother's kitchen, Melba had tried and failed to summon that same feeling of solitude. She was excruciatingly aware of her mother's presence, of her mother coming toward her, her mother lunging across the kitchen in fifteen-pound ankle-weights. Melba shifted her palm gingerly. Part of the snail adhered to her palm and part of the snail adhered to the wall. Melba rubbed her palm against the wall. Her mother was almost upon her, and she rubbed harder, reducing the snail to a dark and textured patch, indistinguishable from the other dark and textured patches on the wallpaper, just as her mother's final lunge brought the toes on her left foot in contact with the dado.

"What are you doing, Melba?" asked Melba's mother, mildly. Melba thought quickly.

"I'm generating static electricity," she said. "Otherwise I fall asleep in the middle of the day. It's perfectly safe."

"Safe!" snorted Melba's mother. "What about Bret Glenn?"

"I don't know about Bret Glenn," said Melba.

"Of course you do," said Melba's mother, her voice vibrating from the exertion of maintaining the lunge. "Bret Glenn!" said Gigi Zuzzo. "He was repairing our television and rubbed his knees on the area rug one too many times. The static discharge made him jump so that he sent his head through the picture tube."

"Did he die?" asked Melba.

"I should say so," said Melba's mother. "You don't see Bret Glenn in town anymore!"

"What did he look like?" asked Melba. "Did he always wear an amulet?"

"No," said Melba's mother. "His hair brushed his collar, ever so lightly. Sometimes you almost thought it wasn't quite reaching, there was no contact, but then, when you got closer, you could see it, you could hear it, Bret Glenn's hair brushing his collar." Her mother gripped Melba's arm and steered her through the kitchen, so they could look down into the sunken room where her mother stored the exercise equipment.

"It happened right there," said Melba's mother, "by the Smith machine. He was so happy! He loved doing favors for friends. He didn't just repair televisions! He dug the septic tank! Sometimes he drove you to elementary school, Melba. I'm surprised you don't remember."

"He didn't die right there," said Melba, uneasily. "Wouldn't he have died somewhere else? In a hygienicized venue? The hospital in Henderson?"

"Dr. Buck was napping upstairs when it happened," said Melba's mother. "But by the time I got him showered and fed and properly awake, there was nothing Dr. Buck could do for Bret Glenn."

"Dr. Buck! He's been to our house!" Melba shrank back against the doorframe. Gigi Zuzzo looked at her with irritation.

"He's been to everyone's house," she said. "He's a doctor. Mayor Bunt made him keys. Sometimes he comes into the house in the night and tiptoes around, just to check on everyone."

"You were telling me about Ann Dump," Melba burst out, desperate to change the subject. "Why does Ann Dump want to lure the snails to the town hall?"

Gigi Zuzzo's lower jaw jutted forward and she dropped into a furious squat.

"Addiction!" she sneered. Melba gasped. She had never joined the clusters of children licking snail and slug trails on the rubber tiles around the condemned Dan Mats & Flooring Emporium, and she had always doubted their reports of hallucinogenic experiences— red foxes playing bouzoukis and long beards growing at tremendous speeds on every face they saw—but she knew at least two of them, Em and Perry Blake, now lived behind the emporium in a hut and did nothing else.

"Ann Dump licks snails?" said Melba.

"Only nitwits lick snails!" snorted Melba's mother. "That Ann Dump is no nitwit. It's the toad she's after. She's infiltrated the reptile trading community with her boxes of snails. Every day, she sends the reptile trading community a fresh box of snails. One of these days, she thinks they'll send her the toad. In the meantime, she doesn't care how many snails run wild in the town hall, what they do to vital records. I've seen the records, Melba! It's as if you don't exist! There's a hole where your name used to be! It's like you've never been born!"

"That Ann Dump," repeated Melba's mother, but Melba suspected that the blame did not rest squarely on Ann Dump. The blame could not be conceived of as a regular polygon, contained and conventionally dimensional. The blame was a bigger, murkier object, with a drifty quality that frightened Melba. The blame hung in the sky over the valley. It was like humidity! Or a curse!

"In Dan, we all live in the shadow of blame," said Melba to herself on her stool in the well-lit bakery. But shouldn't her generation be blameless? Surely they hadn't done anything wrong. And the next generation? The infants? What did Bev Hat's infants have to do with the curse of Dan?

When Melba was a young child, far too young for high school, a group of women had disappeared from Dan. They were older women, old enough to bear some responsibility for Dan's circumstances. Nonetheless, Melba had admired the women. She had enjoyed watching the women eat their meager lunches outside Dan Bras & Girdles No Retail.

In those days, Dan had several businesses in addition to the bakery, and a hosiery district. Mayor Bunt encouraged the production of fine hosiery through financial incentives to hosiers, and quite a few people in Dan had responded to the call. A great deal of hosiery was manufactured in Dan and stored in several warehouses, of which Dan Bras & Girdles No Retail was the largest. Unfortunately, the roads leading into and out of Dan were not stable enough to bear the weight of freighted trucks and it proved impossible to empty the warehouses, or, at least, to empty the warehouses profitably, delivering the goods to points of sale. The warehouses were emptied at a loss. Small barrel fires stoked by tube socks could be seen burning brightly in the hosiery district at night.

Melba was warned by her mother not to visit the hosiery district at night, although other children enjoyed the festive atmosphere and played complicated finger games with elastics cut from the big spools that overflowed the dumpsters.

"You're not like the other children, Melba," said Gigi Zuzzo. "You react poorly to elastics. Whenever you are given a piece of elastic your nose begins to bleed. I blame factors from before your birth. Namely, your abnormally long umbilical cord."

At her mother's mention of her umbilical cord, Melba probed her bellybutton.

"I didn't know about my abnormally long umbilical cord," cried Melba. "Can I see it?"

"I buried it in a secret place and disguised the map," said Gigi Zuzzo, sharply. "You're better off not seeing something like that, Melba."

"You'll never develop normal attachments," sighed Gigi Zuzzo. "We've never been as close as other mothers and daughters, have we

Melba?" But Melba was concentrating and barely heard her mother's question.

"Those years that I had the hiccups," asked Melba. "Was that because of my umbilical cord?"

"It was," said Gigi Zuzzo. "And that's the least of it! The cord's torsional compression in the womb cut off blood flow to your brain and dried out your brainpan. Your brainpan cracked in half! Toxified brain fluid leaked into my blood stream! I was nearly poisoned! I had to drink charcoal every day for a week!"

"The toxic brain fluid," asked Melba. "Did that reach your womb through osmosis? Or was there another process involved?"

"What other process is there?" barked Gigi Zuzzo.

"I don't know," said Melba quietly. "Reverse osmosis, probably."

"No one said anything about processes, reversible or otherwise," said Gigi Zuzzo. "Though the charcoal explains your hairs and your eye color, Melba." Melba's hairs were much blacker than the hairs of her mother, father, and sister, and she had not inherited the blue eyes of her mother and father, having instead dull, protuberant black eyes, which Randal Hans once told her resembled the eyes of a deer with a neck wound.

Melba heeded her mother, and only visited the hosiery district during the day. Outside Dan Bras & Girdles No Retail, the women always seemed to be eating darkened wormy apples. They ate the apples rapidly, producing them one after the other from huge burlap sacks, until a man with a whistle appeared from nowhere, and the women hurried through the metal side-door of Dan Bras & Girdles No Retail, hauling the sacks between them.

As she watched the women from the culvert, Melba would feel the muscles on the sides of her tongue shivering. She longed for just a tiny bite of an oddly-shaped mahogany apple! Until one day Melba Zuzzo could not contain herself. Just as the metal side-door swung shut behind the women, she lunged from the culvert and scuttled across the gravel lot, searching for a discarded apple core. Something dark and slick glinted in the gravel. Melba Zuzzo picked the thing up impulsively and thrust it in her mouth. She recognized the taste! It tasted like when, as a child, she had mashed anchovy in the wall socket and licked the wall socket on all fours, pretending that she was an animal navigating a maze in the service of science. Melba's mouth flooded with saliva. She shuddered. She wondered how the women could maintain their appearances of solid and attractive tidiness while lunching on such apples. The pH of their saliva must be 1! Or 0! What did this saliva do to tooth enamel? Were the women's tongues corroded? For a moment, Melba doubted the sanity of the women, but the moment passed quickly. Melba realized that the dark thing she had discovered was not an apple core, but rather a metal whistle. She spat a hasp and a bit of broken chain into her palm. Suddenly, a man was running toward her. Melba recognized him as the man with the whistle, for even without the whistle, his lips formed a tense repellant O. Melba fled, the man's whistle clamped in her mouth, her breath chirping as it divided inside the whistle, deflecting down into the whistle's dank chamber and up across the whistle's slot. Finally Melba reached a phone booth and ducked inside. She had no desire to keep the whistle in her mouth and removed it immediately.

"What a horrid, strident device," thought Melba Zuzzo angrily as she shoved the whistle in the change slot.

Shortly after this disappointing episode, Dan Bras & Girdles No Retail went out of business. Melba heard that it reopened days later as a travel agency but she never saw anyone coming in or out and weeds grew up thickly in the gravel lot and it became customary for people to drive up to the gravel lot in the night to dump mattresses. What had happened to the women with their sacks of apples?

It was possible that they were sent on a group tour of a foreign land by the travel agency. Melba Zuzzo liked to think of the women eating apples, perhaps beside the Great Wall of China. Eating apples beside the Great Wall of China, a landmark of interest to people in space, the women had a very high chance of being photographed by satellites. Someday Melba hoped to go to a space station, or to Florida, to NASA headquarters. She would eat the astronaut ice cream she had heard so much about and she would buy a satellite photograph of the Earth. Running her magnifying glass along the Great Wall of China, she might at last obtain proof that the women still existed. The women would be unmistakable, crouched in the weeds with their cheeks filled with apples, and Melba knew they could still break her heart with their beauty, even in a photograph taken from the distance of the moon.

The bakery's wall-phone rang and Melba sprang from her stool to answer.

"Bev!" cried a voice. Melba rested her forehead against the wall, cradling the receiver on her shoulder.

"Men lactate," she said, at last. "I've never seen it happen, but they can. I heard from a man who did it. Not at a mere whim!" said Melba hurriedly. "I'm not trying to say that men lactate frivolously. It requires duress, great duress, but it can be done," whispered Melba. "Like on the Oregon Trail. Don't you believe me?"

"Bev!" cried the voice and Melba slowly hung up the phone.

I don't have any obligation to inform Ned Hat, she reminded herself. It's not as though I *am* Bev Hat, no matter what he says. She saw Grady Help's profile moving along the bakery window at head height.

"Grady Help!" she called, running to the door. "Wait!" Grady Help had an open sore on his temple and stopped walking at Melba's cry, looking around dimly, a finger in his ear.

"I'm here," said Melba, rushing up to him. "Right in front of you."

She felt the strangeness of stopping a man like Grady Help on the street.

Grady Help had once been a victim, and as such was not usually spoken to directly. Melba had herself inquired about Grady Help from time to time, asking other townspeople how he was doing and whether he had preferences in daily activities, but facing him now she could not help but feel flustered and importuning. He hasn't been a victim for years, she reminded herself, at least not actively, and so she pressed on.

"Bev Hat is dead," she blurted and wrenched at the waist, burying her face in her hands.

"Well that's not so," said Grady Help gently and Melba uncovered her face. Grady Help's voice was soft and weak but it did not break. It wasn't precisely *firm*, thought Melba, but it held together, possessed of a coagulated quality, like the innocuous cheese Zeno Zuzzo fed her after meals for several months when she was still a schoolgirl. He claimed it was an experiment, although he had never told her the purpose or results. Melba almost smiled at Grady Help's voice; it was a triumph for a former victim, she reasoned, and blushed, not knowing the best way to recognize a former victim's triumph, if tacit approval was suitable or if something more demonstrative was in order, and if the former, how to be certain the tacit approval had registered as such, and if the latter, whether or not the demonstration should center around an impulsive hug, and if yes, how to summon sufficient propulsion and which part of Grady Help's loosely jointed body to encircle. Perhaps she should just grasp his hand in both of hers and press the knuckles to her cheek.

While she hesitated, Grady Help slowly looked Melba up and down.

"Bev Hat isn't dead," he said. "Why I saw her yesterday."

"But that's just it, Grady," said Melba, forgetting his victimization as thoughts of Bev Hat's deadness rushed back. "To know someone is alive you have to see them right now."

Grady Help blinked. "I don't see a lot of people right now, Melba," he said. "In fact, right now I see you. Only you, Melba." Melba spun around, gazed down the empty street. Above the street, a large black bag hanging from a wire snapped in the wind. Melba shuddered. The wind blew harder. The wire was anchored at each end in a metal eyelet driven between bricks in the facades of two opposite-facing buildings, and Melba detected the low sound of the eyelets groaning. Farther down the street, she noticed the flags that usually hung so limply from the cantilevered gaffs alongside the second-story windows of the Dan Hotel leaping about, bright and agitated. The wind was active, moving around, having effects, but it wasn't a person, and Melba looked back at Grady Help. He was right. She was the only one.

Melba opened her mouth then closed it. How did Grady Help know her name? They had watched an animated television program about hot air balloons in adjacent folding chairs in the school auditorium before Grady Help became a victim but he couldn't possibly remember that. He was so different back then, strawberry blond and dressed in neatly pressed chino cloth. Was it that her name was one of the names known to men in Dan? She doubted it. She knew from experience that Melba Zuzzo wasn't a name that appealed to men, not like the names Adele Pear or Stella Duck. Once, when Randal Hans had been her boyfriend, he and Melba had gone stargazing in the swamp. They lay down side by side on a wide plank and looked up at the sky. It was a clear night, all of the stars were displayed, and for a time Melba spoke with Randal Hans about their uneven distribution. In certain regions of the sky, stars clustered thickly, so thickly some mushed together, formed clumps, each double, triple, quadruple the size of a regular star, and with an oozy, bursting brightness. In other regions, darkness dominated, rich and plain, scarcely flecked, another kind of sky altogether. It was as though the night were a batter poorly mixed, a batter into which bagged blueberries had been introduced by an amateur baker, a woman who had never worked at a bakery, who shook the berries from the bag and folded them, still frozen, into the batch, so that two distinct types of muffins resulted from the oven, the one type heavy with fruit, the other dry and light, almost a biscuit.

"But in this instance," said Melba, "the batter is dark like frozen blueberries, and it's the berries that are white, milk-white. There may be such berries," said Melba, "grown in darkness, the bushes hilled over to prevent photosynthesis, or perhaps the berries are grown in caves. Cave berries," said Melba. "Now that I've said it, I feel like I've heard it before. Cave berries." She hoped that Randal Hans would repeat this, like a refrain, and so the conversation might continue, although the conversation would have become something different, something more like a chant.

"Cave berries," said Melba. Randal Hans said nothing. Soon Melba too fell silent. She felt discomfort and fidgeted, but Randal Hans sighed and seemed to settle into the plank as though the plank were a freshly turned bed. Melba turned her head to look at him. Randal Hans was lying perfectly still, smiling encouragingly at the moon.

"I've never been here before," Melba confessed. "Have you?"

"A few times," said Randal Hans. "Wow, I like this plank."

"With other girls?" asked Melba. A damp weight struck her chest and just as suddenly lifted off. She thought it must have been a frog or maybe the feeling had come from *inside* her chest. She almost changed the subject, a question about frogs and hearts rising to her lips—"Do you suppose a frog transplanted in a human chest could perform the heart's functions? They're both muscular lumps, roughly of a size, and if the frog was stimulated with electric impulses . . ."—but said nothing.

"A few other girls," said Randal Hans, at last.

"Were they prettier than me?" asked Melba.

"Now a few of them were," said Randal Hans, reflectively. "But I say that unofficially, Melba. You can't be certain unless you think about girls in a particular way—as composites of discrete features— and then you input data about each feature into a rubric, and I have never been one to use a rubric. Even the word 'rubric' gives me a prickly feeling. I'd rather weed-whack a half-acre of poison celery than prepare an official statement about the prettiness of girls."

"Oh," said Melba, pleased.

"I only asked them to come to the swamp with me because they were the usual girls," explained Randal Hans. "The ones with obvious names that everyone knows. I don't like to point to a girl and say 'Hey you!' It isn't how I was reared."

"Well, that's fine," said Melba Zuzzo, but Randal Hans wasn't finished.

"Your name is difficult, Melba," he said. "It isn't Tara Mint, for example. If you were named Tara Mint, nothing about you would be the same, I mean, at the molecular level. We all vibrate to the frequencies of our names."

"I know that," said Melba.

"Of course you do," said Randal Hans, gently. "And you know that there are some vibrations people respond to positively and there are some they don't. Other creatures may have completely different reactions. Think about dogs. Haven't you noticed the way dogs chase after you? They love you, Melba. I think Melba Zuzzo vibrates in their register."

"Hush," said Melba, because something, an owl perhaps, was flapping by overhead. Perhaps her vibrations were perturbing to owls? She wished she had never mentioned girls to Randal Hans. She never felt quite right when they talked about girls.

"Owls don't give birth in the air ever?" asked Melba, in a rush to change the subject. "Accidentally?" On several occasions, Melba had been struck by eggs while riding her bicycle, but she had never been able to ascertain where the eggs came from, from the sky or the culvert or the surrounding bushes. She began to talk rapidly, recounting where and when she had been struck by each egg, but she could tell by Randal Hans's closed eyes and dreamy smile that he was not participating mentally in the exchange.

"Diana Joy!" cried Randal Hans, starting up. "That's a name that gets around! She was pretty and smart too. But you know the thing about Diana Joy."

"I don't," said Melba.

"She couldn't be close to a man," said Randal Hans. "She worried too much about thermal energy. Men have higher body temperatures than women, and when they're close—pardon this frankness, Melba, I don't know how else to say it—when men and women join together, something happens. The female system is being heated by the male system, and the male system is being cooled by the female system. That's all well and good, but eventually both systems will reach the same temperature and there can't be any further energetic exchange. It's over. Both systems are totally inert."

"I don't . . ." began Melba.

"They die, Melba," said Randal Hans. "That was Diana Joy's problem."

Melba breathed in and out several times, pondering Diana Joy's problem. She was convinced that Randal Hans had brought it up because it was somehow pertinent to the two of them, to Randal Hans and Melba Zuzzo, two energetic systems vibrating side by side on a single plank. This conviction gave her a feeling of satisfaction.

"All of this makes a lot of sense," said Melba slowly. "I don't want us to kill each other, Randal."

"We probably will, but that's okay," said Randal Hans. "I think it takes years of intimacy. As long as a couple doesn't stay intimate for too long, there's really no risk."

He reached out, as though to put his hand on Melba's skirt, but Melba rolled away, right to the edge of the plank, depositing her arm into the water. She was wet to the shoulder but not at all cold. It was a lovely night and the moonbeams made the water less terribly black than one might imagine given its dankness and turbidity. With her nose so close to the water's surface, Melba detected a reassuring odor, fresh tar and fermented cabbage. The plank creaked as Randal Hans rolled after her. Melba felt the heat from his body warming her back.

"There might be a cure someday," said Randal Hans, in frustration.

"Who would cure this kind of thing?" demanded Melba. "Not Dr. Buck!"

"Principal Benjamin was working on the cure for something," said Randal Hans, leadingly. "In the basement of the school."

"I wouldn't know," said Melba and she heard Randal Hans huff, then felt his palms on her shoulders as he pushed off from her, widening the distance between them. They lay in silence, facing away from each other on opposite sides of the plank.

Even though it had seemed to her withholding and mean at the time, Melba was glad then that she had not given herself to Randal

Hans when the opportunity had arisen in the unoccupied car of the funicular device. She loved Randal Hans and didn't want their relationship to end in death or in non-intimacy, but what other options were there? Maybe Melba Zuzzo had a problem too, a problem just like Diana Joy's. She wondered what she wanted with Randal Hans and she thought perhaps something like the muddled closeness one finds between a friendless brother and his friendless sister who live together in an old farmhouse and co-parent an orphan.

Now, Grady Help's keen gaze nicked Melba's reverie, and it rapidly deflated. Her whole head felt saggy and she hadn't the least idea what she'd been thinking about.

"You're wondering how I know your name, aren't you, Melba?" said Grady Help. "I should hope I know your name, if you are the only person alive in Dan."

"But I'm not," protested Melba, weakly. "I never said everyone in Dan was dead, just Bev Hat," but her voice dwindled and all that could be heard was the snapping of the black bag on its wire and the lower groan of the eyelets in brick.

"I'm not surprised that you're playing favorites," said Grady Help bitterly. "You think you're special Melba, that you were made to enjoy extenuating circumstances."

"No, Grady," said Melba.

"Yes, Melba," said Grady Help. "First Principal Benjamin, then Dr. Buck, then the bakery, and now Bev Hat. You've been given everything and you don't even see it! You think there's something else, something better, that's owed to you . . . an apricot-colored poodle you can tie to your waist. You think Hal Drake should machine tiny bearings and attach wheels to your feet and an apricot-colored poodle should pull you all around Dan. You don't even have a hobby, Melba. All you do is wait. I've watched it happen, the waiting. I don't seem lithe, but I fit nicely in the cupboard beneath your sink and I've watched you stand there in your kitchen. Do you know what I've wanted to do? I've wanted to sprinkle the baking soda all around me and douse it with the white vinegar! Do you know what that does?"

"Of course I do, Grady," said Melba.

"Of course I do," echoed Grady Help. "Spoken like Dr. Benjamin's hand puppet!"

Melba gasped. "How did you know about the hand puppet?" Dr. Benjamin had given Melba a hand puppet, a bear with slightly singed fur, one morning in the hall as a prize. But for what? Melba racked her brain. Could Grady Help be right? Maybe she had received prizes for no reason.

"Well I'll tell you, Melba," continued Grady Help. "Baking soda and vinegar makes a chemical reaction. It would blow Dan to Kingdom Come!"

The mention of Kingdom Come reassured Melba, who could see now that Grady Help was raving, that he was perhaps slightly cracked. He wasn't a redheaded person, but he was a victim and as such had often been presented with pamphlets that promoted cult beliefs.

"The phone is ringing," said Melba, "I suppose I should answer it. I know you think it's all fun and games at the bakery, like it's a theme park with lots of rides and attractions, and I spend the day just spinning and spinning in a measuring cup, or shooting weevils in a flour barrel, racking up points that I redeem for specialty goods no one else can get, but you're wrong, completely wrong. It's hard work at the bakery. Sometimes I cry! And when I go home I can't sleep. You're right I'm always waiting. It's because I'm confused about what's happening. Life can't possibly be just what's happening right now. Then you'd be right, it would just be the two of us in the cold street, talking. This would be the whole thing! It's only waiting that makes it more than that. I'd say remembering too, but you can't trust memories. Waiting isn't something you can make up, not in the same way. You have no control over it. I'm glad I'm waiting because I don't want life to be just the two of us. I don't love you, Grady Help. Not because of your sores," said Melba generously. "I have a carbuncle on my earlobe and I know I don't have a figure, not like Bev Hat. I don't love you because love is something you find in someone, you search and search, sometimes in the dark, or blindly, like a miner with a pickaxe or like a star-nosed mole, and you can search all you want in some people and you won't find anything, and the problem might be with you, you're not searching in the right place, but more often than not, there's just no love to find. Some people have it and some people don't. Maybe I have it," whispered Melba. "I've always wished that I did." She took a step closer to Grady Help.

"Do you love me?" asked Melba.

"Damn you," croaked Grady Help and he lurched away from Melba.

Melba watched him go. Grady Help did have a certain dignity! She imagined he might have ascended to a noble profession, working as a male librarian or as a dog trainer, if only he hadn't become a victim instead. The phone was still ringing inside the bakery and Melba scowled.

"Hold your horses!" she said shrilly. It was one of her favorite expressions. She felt the pressure of Dr. Buck's moist, disapproving eyes every time she used it.

"Horses, horses, horses," muttered Melba defiantly as the phone rang on and on. She didn't want to fetch up her skirt and apron and dash to answer and why should she? She wasn't just the bakery phone operator. She had other responsibilities. Melba cast about for something to do, something that fell within her purview as a bakery employee but that required application *outside* the bakery proper. The bakery needed a paint job, but she could hardly begin painting the bakery without rollers and paint. Soap the windows? Melba's eyes lighted on the dough dumpster. Of course! She would drag the dough dumpster out of the street and restore it to its usual position on the rectangle of wet dirt in the weedy alley between the back of the bakery and back of the druggist's. She hooked her fingers on the handle—a greasy metal dowel that deposited a smell in her palm, and a fatty film of the sort that extruded from a hard cheese left on the windowsill—

and tugged. The dumpster was heavy but by tipping it onto its wheels, Melba moved it easily into the alley. She panted slightly as she released the handle and wiped her hands on her apron.

"I wish Ned Hat had seen me do that," thought Melba. Bev Hat certainly wouldn't move dumpsters around if she'd just come back from the dead. Bev Hat had always despised dumpsters. Back when Bev Hat was still Bev Horn, she refused even to empty her own lunch tray. A small girl with pink, naked eyelids and fluffy gray hairs grouped on the center top of her head would empty it for her. No one knew that girl's name. A larger version of her was still seen from time to time near the Hat residence, where perhaps she helped with chores.

Melba liked the alley and stood as comfortably as she could manage given her skeleton, which, no matter what her position, kept her from feeling fully at ease.

Having a human body is like eating a fish for dinner, thought Melba. You have to be so slow and careful. You can't just enjoy yourself. There's always a worry about the bones.

Melba sighed and tried to concentrate on the alley. The bakery vents hummed and dripped. She knew that the dough inside the dumpster was rising, pushing up the lid. There was so much activity in the alley, but not like a footrace or a conversation, where it was expected that you would stagger on and there was always someone to try to get the better of; it was the unaffected and aimless activity of waste processes, not the sort of thing anyone endorsed.

"Hello, alley!" saluted Melba.

A screen door rested up against a lanky junk tree, and there was a cairn of oblong stones that Melba knew to be pestles though she had never seen one used. Between the stones and Melba lay something invisible.

Jelly, thought Melba. Or maybe Mr. Sack was right, maybe it was miasma, something slighter than jelly, viscous and a little nasty, but it wasn't just between the stones and her body, or the dough dumpster and the stones, thought Melba, it was between the stones and the stones, and between her body and her body, and the dough dumpster and the dough dumpster, because the stones and her body and the dough dumpster each existed in other times, in the past and future, and the jelly was what got in the way of seeing all the other stones and all the other Melbas and all the other dough dumpsters; the jelly kept changing its clearness, showing, for example, one Melba, then another, then another; one dumpster, then another, then another.

"I'll never figure it out," thought Melba. "Meanwhile, people keep dying and where they do they go in the jelly? Do they rot in the jelly and make more jelly? Could time be made of people?"

Melba walked slowly from the alley. Inside the bakery the air was warm and fragrant and the phone had fallen silent. Melba heaved a sigh of relief as she settled onto the stool. Sleepily she considered the pretzels on the trays through the glass countertop. Any of them would do for breakfast, with butter and Peggy Shine's orange marmalade, which Melba kept on a special shelf in the walk-in refrigerator. Suddenly the door burst open and Melba sprang to her feet.

"Jumpy aren't you, Melba?" said the man who stood backlit in the doorway. Melba stared at the silhouette.

"Officer Greg," she said, and he approached the counter.

"I'll be the one to name names around here, Melba," said Officer Greg. "If I can even call you Melba." He seemed unwilling to look at Melba head-on and kept his head turned to the side even as he came forward.

"I'm not committing myself to seeing you, Melba," said Officer Greg. "So don't get any ideas that I'll testify on your behalf as an eye-witness."

"You've been talking to Ned Hat," said Melba and she couldn't keep the smug, deductive note from her voice that she knew Officer Greg, like so many officers, found offensive in lay people.

Officer Greg bumped into the counter and stopped coming forward. Melba looked at his profile appreciatively.

"Have you considered becoming a nose model?" she asked.

"I am a police officer, Melba," rapped out Officer Greg, but Melba observed that his nostrils had flared slightly at the compliment.

"Or something more part-time. Donating your nose to science?" she continued, warming to the topic. "It wouldn't take very long and it would do such a world of good. I would donate my own nose but it's an inferior specimen and it seems to me that science should get only the best from people. Think of all science does for us."

"No, Melba, I won't," said Officer Greg. He took a thick roll of clear tape from his pocket. Melba looked at the tape, then followed Officer Greg's gaze. He was looking at the cash register.

"You don't mind if I check for fingerprints," said Officer Greg, scratching the roll of tape lightly with his fingernails, which were long, Melba noted, no doubt for the very purpose.

"It's so difficult to find the end of the tape," she murmured, hoping with the comment to establish a kind of sympathy between them, but Officer Greg flinched. He did not look toward her but Melba saw that his lips trembled with emotion, at least on the left side of his face.

"It's the beginning of the roll of tape," said Officer Greg at last, sighing. "The beginning! Melba, I've championed you to the men of this town, men who claim that you're a succubus, because you've always seemed diurnal to me, decently dressed, and your mother is an athletic woman, but how can I champion you at all if you're going to say such negative things?"

After a pause filled only with the sound of mixers and the light scratching of Officer Greg's fingernails, Melba spoke, painfully aware that her words must sound coy or ungrateful.

"I don't know," she said. "Maybe I don't deserve a champion." Officer Greg did not answer but moved swiftly about the bakery, applying and removing strips of tape to the counter, walls, and ceiling, which he reached using a collapsible police stool that doubled, in its collapsed state, as a cudgel. Melba marveled at this device but said nothing about it. She did not find it easy to speak with police officers. One always wanted something from them, aid or exoneration, or else to be left alone entirely, passed over unnoticed or, if noticed, quickly forgotten, and this made it impossible for one to speak freely, as, say, a rational, disinterested party might be expected to speak in the public sphere. Melba was always imputing some hidden agenda to the comments she made to police officers and this incessant fishing around her own mind for possible motivating factors or subterfuges caused her considerable stress. When faced with a police officer, she would flush and sweat and wring her hands in a manner bound to strike even a near-sighted, kindly, non-inquisitorial person as unreservedly degenerate.

Now, to occupy her hands, the palms of which were already mashed together, fingers jumbled, she became brisk, rising from her stool and pulling out first one tray, then another, scanning the baked goods for desirability.

"Would you like a pretzel?" she asked Officer Greg, and he grunted, labeling the strips of tape and, after punching a hole in each one, slipping them onto a key ring which he clipped to his belt. Melba selected three pretzels and wrapped them carefully in wax paper before nestling them in a large white paper bag. She passed them over the counter to Officer Greg who reached out for them, head still turned to the side, opening and closing his hand like a pincers several times on empty air before Melba could aim the bag between his fingers.

Officer Greg sighed, his profile surprisingly eloquent for the profile of a police officer at that hour of the morning. It wasn't just the above-average nose, but the long drape of the eyelid, which was thin and trapezoidal, nothing puffy or stubby about it.

"My gut tells me you're not supernatural, Melba," said Officer Greg. "I don't quite believe you're an employee . . ."

"But I *am* an employee," broke in Melba. "Leslie Duck is my boss. What else could I be?"

"I'm going to run these prints and we'll see," said Officer Greg. "You could be a lot of things. A wife, a mother, a safe-breaker, a patient . . ."

"I'm not!" protested Melba.

"Well maybe you're a victim, then . . ." continued Officer Greg and Melba gasped.

"A victim! Like Grady Help?"

Officer Greg's fine eyelid quivered. "Who told you Grady Help was a victim?"

Melba swallowed.

"Everyone knows it," she said. "It was a pillow fight, wasn't it? He was suffocated during a pillow fight at Dan Elementary during the annual slumber party. I almost think I was there, or nearby anyway, asleep in the bleachers."

"Grady Help is not a victim, Melba," said Officer Greg.

"What is he then?" asked Melba eagerly. She leaned forward, letting her eyes drop down the ledge of Officer Greg's brow and skim over the sophisticated slope of his nose again and again, deriving a breathless pleasure from it. She hadn't expected confidences from Officer Greg!

"He's a renter, Melba," said Officer Greg and Melba jerked her hands apart and slammed one fist on the counter.

"Why yes!" she cried. "He is!" Just a few days before, Melba had run into her mother while wandering the weedy verges of the public golf course and her mother had taken the opportunity to denounce Grady Help in exactly those terms.

"Men like Grady Help are old enough to be fathers, but what are they?" Gigi Zuzzo had said. "Renters! They get together and play tabletop games. All their money goes to tables. What's the difference between a table and a house?"

Melba had not answered her mother. She had often thought that a table was in fact like a house, but a more wonderful house, a miniature house created especially for just one person. How she dreamed of sitting beneath a table, curling up in the gently dipping curve of a trestle foot, sucking a pistachio, the floor-length vinyl tablecloth closing her in on all sides.

Gigi Zuzzo waited, tapping her fingernails on her front teeth. Finally she could wait no more.

"I'll tell you," said Gigi Zuzzo. "Property taxes! A man who owns a table doesn't have to pay property taxes. If everyone owned a table instead of a house, we wouldn't have roads. We wouldn't have schools either. Who do you think drove away your precious Principal Benjamin?" Gigi Zuzzo spat a golf tee she had been holding in her mouth like a toothpick and went on with clearer speech. "Men like Grady Help, that's who. Your father Zeno Zuzzo is almost a man like Grady Help," said Gigi Zuzzo. "Do you know what the difference is between your father and Grady Help?"

Melba shook her head cautiously.

"Me!" cried Gigi Zuzzo. "I turned your father into your father, but otherwise he was Grady Help. Whenever I kicked him out of the house he reverted back into his Grady Help-like state, but worse, because he didn't rent anything. He moved into Pike's Ditch and slept under the footbridge."

Melba nodded, less cautiously. She remembered when her father moved into Pike's Ditch, an increscent gouge rumored to be a natural formation that divided the Dan junkyard from the retirement home. Gigi Zuzzo seemed much happier with Zeno Zuzzo living there. As soon as he left, she'd moved Melampus into the master bedroom and given up sleep. Giving up sleep, claimed Gigi Zuzzo, had an energizing effect and built muscle mass. She had given up sitting as well, and whenever Melba came through the door after an outing Gigi Zuzzo was standing behind it, already speaking. Melba went on many outings in those days. She would visit her father in Pike's Ditch and together they passed the glad hours. Zeno Zuzzo showed Melba how he occupied himself throwing knives into a pile of tires and also imitated birdcalls. Melba was impressed by the birdcalls and once she had made the mistake of demonstrating to her mother the different trills and chirps. Gigi Zuzzo's face had darkened as Melba fluted out the lovely little sounds.

"I don't suppose your father was too busy chirping to tell you about Shane Joseph?" Gigi Zuzzo asked.

"Shane Joseph," Melba murmured. She remembered a man who had come as a speaker to Dan Elementary. He had long hair and wore an ace bandage on his wrist. He had told a story:

Once upon a time, he—Shane Joseph—was struck by lightning while playing guitar on his porch in a droning, staticky drizzle. The guitar was incinerated, and he had not replaced it. He had not even mourned it. The lightning strike had destroyed, for him, not only that particular guitar, but all guitars. The very idea of guitar had been erased from his consciousness. He knew the word "guitar" but the word corresponded to nothing, to a void that then filled with the sounds guitars had masked. Without guitar, Shane Joseph was able to listen at last to the music of the moss, the moss that seemed so much a part of Dan, always at hand, always underfoot, mantling stones and bricks, shingles and boards, tree trunks and porch furniture, that no one suspected its alien origins; no one, with the exception of Shane Joseph, heard it sing of its journeys, of its spores that had traveled light years through interstellar space; no one heard it sing of the world's end, of the sub-aquatic cities the survivors would build beneath the risen seas and of the glorious governance of those cities; no one, with the exception of Shane Joseph, and whatever young people might someday be taught to join him in the erasure of guitar from their consciousnesses, opening in its place the void that would be filled with songs of creation and destruction, the songs of the moss, thank you—and as Shane Joseph finished speaking, Principal Benjamin stood and dimmed the lights. In the ensuing silence, he switched on the overhead projector, showing architectural drawings of a black granite pyramid in the place of the school music trailer. Shortly thereafter, the school music trailer was demolished, but the construction of the pyramid was never completed, and rather than functioning as a power station, it seemed, in its half-finished state, the closest thing to a tomb Principal Benjamin had been accorded. Melba sighed. The memory of Shane Joseph brought her pain. Shane Joseph.

"He wears an ace bandage?" she said.

"Not that Shane Joseph!" Gigi Zuzzo snorted. "This Shane Joseph was a vagrant. Vagrants move about on foot, but they also need their arms. Vagrants climb water towers and they scale other things too. Cabooses. Well, Shane Joseph learned the hard way about birds."

Melba listened with interest. She had a great fondness for birds. Whenever the opportunity presented itself, she would run up the hill behind the house and play dead upon a rocky eminence, hoping to lure a hungry raptor from the air. After a few hours, supine, staring at the pointillated blue and white of the sky, she would experience restless motion in her limbs and roaring in her ears, and hurry home for freezer pastries and milk. But she would always return to the eminence, dreaming of the young hawk that would descend from the sky to stick its beak into her viscera. She would start up, catching it unawares, and tame it, teaching it to ride upon her forearm, and, in leather gauntlet, she would journey through life providing a perch for a compact, responsive friend whose physical and emotional maintenance would become her great calling. Gigi Zuzzo, however, pronounced the word "bird" so as to emphasize its tinny, brittle quality, alerting Melba to its irreconcilability with the word "friend," which she knew had a warm center, like runny caramel in a chocolate square.

"Shane Joseph's vagrancy brought him to Pike's ditch," said Gigi Zuzzo, "but he was only passing through. He didn't intend to stay there. He was a true vagrant, not the type that's always looking for some excuse to settle down. But your father invited him to spend the night beneath the footbridge, and Shane Joseph agreed. The next thing . . . Kablooey!"

"Kablooey," echoed Melba.

"Bird droppings are flammable!" cried Gigi Zuzzo. "Your father treads lightly. He had no problems skimming over the bird droppings that had accumulated under the footbridge. But vagrants shuffle, Melba. They have a shuffling gait, and they tend to take great big breaths, like this, Melba," Gigi Zuzzu expanded her impressive diaphragm. "It's a tendency vagrants have. They think it demonstrates that they are unconfined. These breaths are expressive of the vagrant's sense of freedom, do you understand? Now combine these deep breaths with kicked up bird droppings, rum vapor, and a stubby cigar and what do you get?"

"Kablooey?" whispered Melba.

"Kablooey!" It was obvious that Gigi Zuzzo wished she had a small paper lunch bag she could blow up and punch explosively into a wall. She looked longingly at the milk carton Melba held in her hand, but Melba shook it up and down to indicate that it was as yet too full of milk.

"Your father is lucky Officer Greg and I understand one another," said Gigi Zuzzo, "or your father would very likely have been accused of vigilantism, or have had his name added to a registry of second-degree murderers and been forced to perform community services, landscaping, decorating paper plates for senior lunches, running the flu clinic, helping Dr. Buck check children for scoliosis and lice." The conversation ended then, because Gigi Zuzzo, recalling Melba's curvature, had forced her facedown onto a fitness ball, and spent the remainder of the evening pulling alternately on her left arm and right leg.

Now, in the bakery, Melba noticed her left shoulder and right hip listing in opposite directions, no doubt the result of her uncorrected S-curve, and she wished she had been more stoic regarding her mother's ministrations. Her mother's words ran dizzy laps in her head and she looked at Officer Greg with wonderment.

"Is it true you understand my mother?" asked Melba. Her question came almost too late. Officer Greg was leaving. She could tell by the way he'd drawn up the corner of his mouth, lifting the bag of pretzels to brace against his chest. Officer Greg spun toward her but, remembering that he did not intend to look at her full on, he overshot the mark, pivoting to present her with his other profile, this one jowly, not nearly as debonair. He blinked rapidly, staring out through the bakery window, squinting even, as though trying to read the backwards lettering frosted on the front of the glass.

"That case has been solved, Melba," said Officer Greg in a light tone designed to counteract the intimacy of the disclosure. "I won't reopen it. You should worry about yourself. There's nothing secure about your position. I can't think of a single person who would vouch for anything about you. You say Leslie Duck is your boss, but I don't have any records of Leslie Duck's being anyone's boss. Leslie Duck is a bachelor. The last I heard of Leslie Duck he was moving to the coast to start a banana plantation."

Melba's mouth opened and closed. It had been quite some time since she'd laid eyes on Leslie Duck. And he *had* been talking about bananas!

"Let me tell you something about bananas," Leslie Duck had said. "They're blanks, Melba. Sterile! Isn't that wonderful? There's so much fecundity in fruit form. It disgusts me, all the juices and seeds. I spit them! Pah! The banana is different. There's something self-contained about a banana. I don't just mean the peel, which has a prophylactic quality. The banana itself is reserved, dry and continent, no leaks. You can really hold onto a banana. You can eat it or you can keep it by your side, in your pocket, or in a banana pouch slung from your belt." He showed Melba his banana pouch.

"Is that rabbit fur?" she asked.

"Badger," said Leslie Duck, thumbing the mussed hairs. What else had he said? Melba could not remember. Surely nothing about leaving Dan for good? She glanced around the bakery. Everything seemed in order, not at all as though the owner had abdicated, severing the employer-employee relation, transforming the bakery into an acephalous establishment, a chaotic zone of rogue interactions and escalating depravity. The rubberized maps were in place by the customer entrance; the refrigerator was stocked with bottles of chocolate milk and orange soda; the napkin dispenser on the counter bulged with napkins. Officer Greg had left a piece of tape on the brass drawer of the enormous cash register, but police officers left tape in all kinds of places; it meant nothing.

"Am I trespassing?" asked Melba in bewilderment. "I thought I was working."

Officer Greg looked almost pitying. "I'll get to the bottom of it," he promised. "That's what I do. I'm like a submersible. Just remain calm and go through your day as you would normally, as though you were Melba Zuzzo, daughter and bakery employee."

"I'm a sister too!" Melba burst out.

Officer Greg shook his head. "Calm, Melba. No wild claims. No histrionics. I'm taking the evidence to the station." He paused, shifting the paper bag in his arms.

"Hmmm," he said, looking down at the bag with real fondness, stroking a crinkle with his fingertip. "Melba, you know, I do hope you work here. I'd hate to consider this bag contraband. Now, what about the Danish with the cheese?" Numbly, Melba plucked a cheese Danish from its tray with the metal tongs and thrust it toward Officer Greg. He opened the bag and Melba dropped the Danish inside.

"Thank you, Melba," said Officer Greg, patting the bag, staring wistfully at a point on the wall above her head. Leslie Duck had allowed Melba to decorate that wall. Melba had taped up recipe cards, each showing a brightly colored image of a hot assembled food. Melba had unearthed the recipe cards while digging for pleasure in Hissy Mary's famously unkempt lawn. The recipe cards were well-preserved, stacked inside a chafing dish enveloped in black plastic. Melba pulled off the plastic and lifted the lid. Expecting eggs, which she knew were occasionally interred, not by hens but by connoisseurs, sometimes for hundreds of years, she had been delighted to find the recipe cards instead. She had even knocked on Hissy Mary's door to share news of her discovery. Luckily, Hissy Mary did not come quickly to the door. Standing there on the doorstep, Melba had time to reconsider. She reconsidered, turning and running from the door. She ran cradling the chafing dish, which bruised the insides of her arms, and she forgot the shovel and sweater in her haste. She had liked the sweater. It had nubs all over and looked casual on regular days and fancy on holidays. The shovel, though, she thought, was just as well abandoned. Twice in the night, sleepwalking from the house, she had woken behind the juniper bush to find Zeno Zuzzo using the shovel to beat things no longer moving. He swore on his honor that the things had, until the moment of Melba's appearance, in fact been moving. They had been moving aggressively, and Zeno Zuzzo had been acting in self-defense. Or had he told her he had performed the deeds for hire? Melba could not remember. Either way, Zeno Zuzzo did not enjoy resorting to the shovel. She remembered he had said as much—"Melba, do you think I enjoy resorting to the shovel in this way? I do not. I do not enjoy this resorting"— and she supposed he would be grateful the shovel was gone.

Melba wished she wasn't remembering the shovel, not with Officer Greg so close. She didn't think she'd done anything wrong, but of course she wouldn't know. She wasn't an officer. She resisted the urge to look behind her. Officer Greg seemed to be studying the recipe cards, perhaps anticipating the criminal applications of either the cards themselves or the various ingredients they listed. At last, Officer Greg shook his head slightly, rocking the bag.

"Carry on," he said to Melba. "Nothing's been proven. How do you spell 'dormouse'?"

"D-O-R-M-O-U-S-E," said Melba.

"Interesting," said Officer Greg. "Very interesting. Most civilians would get dormouse wrong."

Melba considered explaining. I think a lot about vermin, she could say. Officer Greg's jowl was quivering.

"Bev Hat was quite the speller, wasn't she?" he said. "Don't answer! You don't have to say anything else. Not yet. I've already had Bev Hat's report cards delivered to the station. We'll see about her spelling." He jammed his arm roughly into the bag and removed the Danish. Melba looked away, but glanced back in time to see Officer Greg opening his mouth wide, inserting the Danish to a considerable depth, and tearing it fiercely with his teeth. For a long moment, he chewed.

"You claimed this was a Danish?" he asked, sniffing at the glistening, gibbous object now balanced on his palm. Melba wrung her hands, mind racing. Soon her thoughts were all behind her, distant and small, impossible to distinguish from one another. Had she claimed that the baked good in Officer Greg's hand was a Danish? Hadn't he been the one to call it a Danish? With his free hand, Officer Greg manipulated his roll of tape, unspooling a long strip. He wrapped the Danish with grim, exacting motions. No trace of friendliness softened any plane or angle of the features presented to Melba's anxious gaze.

"Don't leave town," said Officer Greg. He was looking at the taped-up Danish in his hand, but Melba knew he meant her, whoever she might prove to be. After he banged out through the door, she sank down upon her stool.

The phone rang and she leapt up, lifted the receiver, and let it drop heavily, severing the connection.

"There!" said Melba viciously. Would Bev Hat do anything so discourteous? Mothers hardly hung up on morning callers! Mothers seemed to expect people to call in the mornings. They coveted these calls: calls from friends who wanted to report on some developmental benchmark of interest to mothers, or calls from older, informed people who kept abreast of the prevailing wisdom on hazards and could advise mothers accordingly. Often mothers called each other in the morning to discuss achievements or to hint that an alternative to a popular consumer good could be made by hand. Why, try keeping a mother away from a ringing phone, from the prospect of an engrossing conversation!

How do I know so much about mothers? thought Melba, and shivered. Surely she hadn't known so much yesterday?

But is something different about me? thought Melba. Or is it just a different morning? Melba tried to think about the morning. What kind of morning was it? Damp, but that was the weather, not the morning. Unpleasant, but that feeling—that feeling of being not entirely pleased—that was her feeling, not the feeling of the morning. The morning did not feel anything. The morning was precisely that: unfeeling.

A monster, thought Melba Zuzzo.

The bakery was hot, stifling, but Melba shivered again. Before morning, it was night, thought Melba, but what kind of night? She tried to remember the night. She had heard a long, lonely hoot outside her window, and finally, unable to sleep, she had gone downstairs to cook a tiny pancake. Meanwhile, Bev Hat had died and Ned Hat had become an old man. Grady Help had crept into her house and crouched beneath her kitchen sink, and maybe Dr. Buck too, and Hal Conard had made his rounds through the streets of Dan.

Nothing can really be known about the morning or the night, thought Melba. I suppose that's why we have dates. The numbers make tiny equations and we can learn the numbers and feel like we've settled something. Melba, not for the first time, marveled at the strangeness of morning and night sharing a date when they were so palpably distinct.

If Melba were mayor of Dan, she would see that this was changed. It would be her first initiative. Day and night would be divided, no longer lumped together by the chuckleheaded mandate of the calendar. The change was bound to be popular; it was reasonable, and it would serve to speed things up—dates flying past, two or maybe even four dates in a twenty-four hour period—so one no longer had to drag along from midnight to midnight, forced to consider an experience so protracted and yet so disjunctive as a single unit.

But when before did I ever hanker for a political voice? Melba touched her throat gently, then pinched and wiggled her windpipe, rather roughly.

I'm so tired of thinking, she thought. The only distraction is small bodily manipulations and I'm tired of those too. She looked with hope at the bakery door. The bakery door banged open. In walked Don Pond.

Thank—, thought Melba.

Don Pond was the bakery's first customer every day, but he never boasted.

"It's luck, Melba," Don Pond had told her, long ago, back when they were still assessing one another's prospects as people. Melba had just handed him his bags of garlic sticks and psyllium husk brownies and listened politely.

"I don't move faster than other men," Don Pond had said, "and I don't wake up any earlier. I can't say I'm more deserving than they are, either. In fact, many would say I'm less deserving."

Soon a precedent was established. Don Pond would always linger after purchasing his baked goods, making modest claims and waving a garlic stick so that salt and chips of toasted garlic fell onto the counter. He and Melba would lick their fingertips and press them down on the counter, returning their fingers to their mouths and sucking off the savory crumbs. Melba came to enjoy these interludes with Don Pond, except on occasion, when Don Pond was in a mood and his modesty became taxing.

"I've caused a lot of suffering, Melba," Don Pond would confess.

"Oh Don, you're in a mood," Melba would interrupt but he would not be put off. When Don Pond was in one of his moods, he interrogated himself ruthlessly, finding fault after fault, and nothing Melba said to encourage leniency made any impression. Just the other week he had stomped into the bakery and Melba could tell from his patchily shaven head and bare, goose-pimpled arms that he was in the throes of a mood the likes of which he had never before inflicted upon her.

"I've caused a lot of suffering, Melba," he began. "I mean physical suffering! To others. In podiatry class, I discovered a splinter in the sole of a classmate's foot, and I dug for the splinter with a needle, dug deeply, until I had exhausted myself. Can I tell you a secret, Melba, something I've never told anyone?"

"Is it because you see me as a person of little consequence?" asked Melba. She retreated through the swinging door into the back of the bakery as she said it, overcome by emotion. She opened and slammed the walk-in refrigerator door so Don Pond would think she was checking on the pitchers of eggs. The cold blast of air felt good against her face and neck. Melba liked Don Pond. She felt close to him when they laughed together, licking their fingers and tasting the pungency of lightly charred garlic: such a flooding, intimate taste to share with someone before most people were even awake. Then he had to spoil it by bringing up secrets, secrets he would only tell to a nobody. But maybe he didn't see her as a nobody, maybe he saw her as Melba Zuzzo, and, as such, peculiar and unassociated, unlikely to share his secrets with others.

She pushed back through the door and marched to the counter to face Don Pond, who had pulled several paint squares from his shirt pocket and was holding them up in different combinations.

"Do you see me as a person alone, isolated from intercourse?" demanded Melba, blushing.

"Intercourse, Melba?" said Don Pond delicately, stacking the paint squares and sliding them back into his pocket.

"Dealings," said Melba. "You know how secrets spread through Dan," said Melba. "It's like wildfire! Or butter! What do you call that if not intercourse? But sometimes intercourse skips a person, an isolated person, a person so unlike other people that that person is on the brink of extinction. Is that how you see me? As a person skipped by intercourse? On the brink of extinction?"

"I think there would be signs if you were on the brink of extinction," said Don Pond, shocked out of his modesty by her outburst. "Think about it, Melba. There would be special protections. You wouldn't be allowed to just come and go, all day and all night, riding around Dan on a bicycle, springing animals from traps. You'd be kept in a special facility until you reproduced, and not with just anyone, with a family member, Melba. I don't mean biological family," said Don Pond quickly as Melba recoiled. "I mean a person who shares your most jeopardized quality. Do you even know what quality that would be?"

"I am psychic," said Melba Zuzzo.

Don Pond whistled. He had a very nice, full whistle, so nice that his whistling might be considered a quality in its own right. But Don Pond did not stop to comment on his whistle. He was focused on Melba. Melba stood with her arms straight at her sides while he admired her.

"Well, that's it, then, Melba," said Don Pond. "Psychic. Wow." He shook his head. "I don't suppose anyone knows about that, or I'd have heard. It's only fair that I tell you my secret, not because of intercourse, just because you told me one of yours." He shut his eyes. For a long time he didn't speak.

"There was no splinter in my classmate's foot," he said at last. "Oh, I showed her a splinter alright, but it was a pencil shaving from my own pocket. I dug in her foot purely for my own gratification. I've slapped people, too, Melba, hundreds of times, during mosquito season. 'Hold still,' I'd say. 'There's a mosquito.' Then bam! But do you think the mosquitoes were really there?"

"Not always," said Melba, generously.

"That's right," said Don Pond, slowly. "Not always. So you see," he continued, "I don't deserve anything, not compared to people who've never slapped for no reason. I don't know why I'm so favored in this life. It's not in reward for my sterling character! I suppose, Melba, we were all of us given paths to walk in life, and some paths are lucky paths that lead you where you want to go in advance of the hordes. Shortcuts, if you will."

"Your house is very close to the bakery," Melba agreed.

"I don't know if it is," said Don Pond. "But my *path* is shorter. Luck has nothing to do with where a man builds his house. That's a zoning issue. I'm talking about getting from A to B. What if there's an ocean between A and B? It would take you a little while to cross that ocean, wouldn't it Melba?"

"It would," said Melba.

"Well there is no ocean between me and the bakery," said Don Pond, and let the matter rest there.

Now Melba almost cried out with relief as Don Pond strode across the bakery. To face Don Pond across the counter—surely this was normal! He did not look at all tentative in his dark knit cap and earring.

"Thank you, Don!" gasped Melba extending her hands. Don Pond grasped them. His hands were ice cold and Melba noticed that his wrists, which extended past the cuffs of his dark jacket, were a vivid pink.

"You're cold!" she observed.

"The temperature's dropping out there," said Don Pond. "I almost turned back several times." He paused, perseveringly. Then he tightened his grip on her hands. Melba braced herself for the outburst.

"Officer Greg was here!" cried Don Pond, a catch in his voice.

"He didn't buy anything," Melba said loyally. "He didn't come in the capacity of a customer. There haven't been any other customers, I swear it, Don."

"He left holding a bag . . ." Don Pond's large, glaucous eyes began to shine. "He had what could have been a Danish in his hand . . ."

"Evidence," said Melba. She realized Don Pond was trembling. His teeth chattered within his trim beard.

"Hold on." Melba pulled her hands free and hurried through the swinging door into the depths of the bakery, turning all of the ovens as high as they would go. Then she opened the back door, and, returning to the front of the bakery, opened the front door as well, propping it with a gallon can of chestnuts.

"We'll see what that does," she said with satisfaction. "I don't expect it will warm the whole of Dan, but, then again, it may. For now, come around the counter. We'll go into the back and stand in front of the ovens."

"I couldn't," said Don Pond. "Even as the first customer, I don't deserve that kind of privilege. It isn't authorized."

"Oh," Melba blinked. She found his attitude provoking and didn't like this newly revealed aspect of his character. It seemed to her that Don Pond couldn't be resisting out of modesty alone. What if Don Pond wasn't simply modest? What if he was, in fact, some kind of stickler?

Melba tried not to hold it against him, but it was difficult. Zeno Zuzzo loathed sticklers and Zeno Zuzzo was an influential man, a man with whom it behooved Melba to share beliefs. Zeno Zuzzo did not like to name names but he did enjoy speaking knowledgeably about types, or worse, maintaining an ominous silence about the type in question.

Melba remembered a particular episode.

"Look!" Zeno Zuzzo had exploded, pointing out a large and a small woman loitering outside the town hall, perhaps eager to be viewed by a passing committee. Melba followed his finger, straining to make out details but only reconfirming the relative largeness and smallness of the figures, which struck her suddenly as very funny.

"They're different sizes!" She giggled and Zeno Zuzzo glanced at her approvingly, then gave a brief hard guffaw.

"Do you see the ears?" he asked. "Those women are conspiring, always conspiring. Why else would they need ears set so close to their mouths? They're whispering things to themselves, Melba. They're stirring themselves up. They won't be satisfied until they assassinate, someone, anyone. If you can drop a person like that with a well-aimed rock, you should do it, before they have a chance to attack. If you don't notice the ears until they're upon you, prepare for close combat. Soap in a sock is handy."

Melba nodded, fingering her own ears. The earlobes were not attached, but then again, they were not nearly as long and loosely formed as her father's. Zeno Zuzzo had extraordinarily long earlobes and his ears were set far back on his head. He was very proud of his ears and emphasized their shape and position with his signature haircut, the Belmondo. No other man in Dan was as well-suited to his Belmondo as was Zeno Zuzzo.

"Someday somebody should write a book about me," Zeno Zuzzo often remarked. When Melba was a student at Dan Elementary, Zeno Zuzzo would say it while reviewing Melba's report card, which always indicated satisfactory performance in the literary arts: penmanship and spelling. Zeno Zuzzo would nod meaningfully at the report card and wink. Zeno Zuzzo was very good at winking.

"A wink is a friendly gesture with a little something extra," Zeno Zuzzo explained to Melba. "A little oomph. Like when a man calls another man 'sweetheart' then riddles him with bullets between the groin and knee." Before leaving Dan Elementary, Mrs. Burr had told Melba's class that a wink was a wizard's kiss, but Melba knew better than to repeat anything Mrs. Burr said to her father. Besides, in this case, it was irrelevant. Melba Zuzzo could not wink.

But on the subject of sticklers, Zeno Zuzzo maintained a chilling silence.

"Don't get me started about sticklers," was all he would say, then he would sink onto his haunches, stroking his lower lip with his thumb, his dark brow beetling, and Melba would back away, sensing the restrained malevolence and understanding implicitly the lowliness of the stickler, his lack of all human worth, and, worse, his inability to contribute to the natural world, the vegetable and mineral kingdoms to which all beings who are not sticklers tithe.

Don Pond, a stickler? She wouldn't believe it. Swiftly, Melba changed the subject.

"I had an idea for a new kind of pastry," she said, brightly. "Instead of using ingredients, I would use quintessence. I would combine the quintessence of multiple things, quail, I think, for one, and custard, and I'd make a glaze of course and sprinkle nonpareils on top, either whole nonpareils or their quintessence, I'm not sure."

Don Pond's expression did not change, but Melba reassured herself that his face was still quite cold; she couldn't expect it to flex readily just because she'd said something fascinating. She gathered garlic sticks and brownies and presented Don Pond with a large bag.

"Thank you, Melba," said Don Pond. He took the bag and held it awkwardly, and Melba watched him closely, moistening her finger with her tongue. She waited impatiently for him to open the bag and begin to speak, rapidly, self-loathingly, waving a garlic stick from which salt and garlic chips would shower down. She held her moistened finger at the ready. But Don Pond did not open the bag. Don Pond looked around the bakery as though he had no status there at all, as though he were not the first customer, as though he were not even finite, and therefore had no ascertainable value whatsoever.

"I've been talking with some of the other men," said Don Pond. "Melba, you're not safe here in the bakery. What's that on the floor? Never mind. Don't look. It's better not to look. Listen, Melba, I'm not blaming you. Some employees try to get themselves killed at work. They say they're fetching the stepladder to change a light bulb and the next thing you know, they've let the ceiling fan take their heads off. That's not you! What's happening here is beyond your control. Melba, you need to leave the bakery at once."

"I wouldn't want to say that you and the other men are wrong, Don," said Melba. "But I know that I'm safe in the bakery. Once I cracked an egg on the side of the mixing bowl and a chick fell out. That was startling and I felt shaky for some time afterwards, but I finally came to terms with it and accepted that there's an explanation. I mean, eggs are supposed to be eggs and not chickens, but there is a point in the genesis of eggs and chickens when they're the same thing. In the bakery, I have things I do when I feel afraid and they really help. I'll show you."

Melba ran through the swinging door. In the depths of the bakery, the air had turned hot and acrid. Melba squinted in the dull orange light and sniffed. Something inside the ovens was definitely burning. The top shelf of the oven billowed smoke. Melba finished squinting and didn't pause a second longer. She considered herself a veteran of such situations, situations in which nothing can be saved. She had no qualms about allowing whatever it was inside the oven to burn itself off. She rushed past the oven with her hands over her nose and mouth. No, she would not open the oven door. Why create a mess out of false sentimentality? She pulled a heavy bucket from beneath the long table and struggled back toward the front of the bakery through the smoke. A moment later, she was heaving the bucket around the counter, dropping it by Don Pond's feet. She yanked off the lid.

"Salt," panted Melba. She ducked behind the counter, rummaging, and returned holding a wooden dowel. Crouching beside the bucket, she thrust the dowel into the salt. For several quick, shallow breaths, she stirred the salt in the bucket with a wooden dowel, then she stirred for several slow, deep breaths, and, finally, she released the dowel and sat motionless on the bakery floor, her elbow in the bucket, the top four inches of the dowel pressing against her inner arm. She looked up at Don Pond. He was looking at the ceiling.

"You don't even have a ceiling fan," he said.

"Don," said Melba. "Maybe I can't trust this sensation, but I feel wonderful right now, warm and confident. My palms are even tingling. I couldn't feel half so good if I were somewhere else, if I weren't in the bakery, if I were in my bedroom, for example, thrashing on the floor between rolled-up balls of tights. Even if I kept buckets of salt in my bedroom, and installed a tower of ovens, I'd always feel more imperiled in my bedroom than in the bakery."

The essential nature of Melba's bedroom differed from the essential nature of the bakery in ways she couldn't quite pinpoint, but that brought her vivid apprehensions of impending doom.

"If I had to describe my bedroom to someone, not to a future tenant, to a disinterested party, to you Don, I would say that my bedroom has a demented, disconsolate nature. Have you ever discovered voles in your pillowcasings?"

"Of course, Melba," said Don Pond, but he was still looking at the ceiling, shifting from foot to foot.

"I've made you uncomfortable!" cried Melba. "I shouldn't be talking about my bedroom, but Don, it's so frightening. Maybe you and the men are right about the bakery. Maybe I don't notice how unsafe it is because I'm always comparing it to my bedroom, and the bakery is a kind of Elysian Field compared to my bedroom, not to sound snobbish," added Melba, who could be shy about her admiration for the classical world.

Don Pond was no longer looking up. His head was sinking between his shoulders and he looked stricken. Melba knew she had to stop speaking. She pressed her lips together and clutched the dowel with both hands, stirring as she mastered herself.

There was something essentially upsetting about her bedroom, she thought, assured by the pressure of the dowel on her palms. It was as though her bedroom had been built on the site of an ancient burial ground. The walls were a sickening, fertilized color, lush and waxy. The carpet fibers broke easily between her fingers, just as hairs would break after centuries of neglected grooming.

Melba disliked the way bakery customers white-gloved the bakery, fingering the refrigerator, the counter, the walls, the window, and even the linoleum, zinging her with their haughty observations about dusts, greases, and molds, but at least the bakery customers usually had the good manners to hurry, shouting orders as they charged the counter and rebukes as they barreled out the door. There was something affirming about their outrage. The bakery's customers seemed to harbor a belief in standards. They seemed to believe that excellence existed, that it was attainable, by Melba herself, if she just applied herself more vigorously and with greater attention to sanitary procedure. The visitants to her bedroom, on the other hand, were silent and unhurried and their abuses could not be attributed to ideals. These visitants circled her bed in rotting smocks, displaying flesh of disturbing translucency, brindled here and there with rope burns. They often huddled on Melba's stomach, compressing her diaphragm with heels and clammy buttocks. That would never happen in the bakery! Her bedroom was a different order of place, a place that emanated malignancy, and Melba had wondered on occasion if this emanation fell under the purview of her landlord, Mark Rand, or if the emanation was beyond his jurisdiction.

Melba's pulse hammered so hard in her temples that she jerked up, gripping the dowel as hard as she could manage, swirling the salt until her palms chafed and she turned away from the bucket, scooting to lean her back firmly against the counter.

"This can't go on," said Don Pond, shaking his fist, and for the first time Melba noticed that his inflexible features had a steely quality. "If it were just me who thought so, I'd never say," continued Don Pond, "but there's a quorum, and because I'm the first customer, the men wanted me to be the one to tell you. I told them I didn't ask to be first customer, or even try in particular, and I never make much of it. How do you even know that I hold that distinction? I asked the men, and they gave no satisfactory answer. But I assure you they knew. Listen, Melba, no one would suggest you go to your bedroom and sleep, not now. But why don't you come to my house, Melba?" Suddenly, Don Pond stiffened, and Melba leapt to her feet.

"What is it?" she asked.

"Dr. Buck is right outside," whispered Don Pond hoarsely. "I saw him through the window."

"Dr. Buck! But what's he doing there?" Melba ducked down again, pretending to tie her shoe.

"He's jumping up and down," said Don Pond. "He's rubbing his hands together."

Melba rose but not to her full height. Bending sharply at the waist, she scurried around the counter, then flattened herself against the wall.

"He's stamping his feet," said Don Pond. "He's swaying his hips. Have you ever seen anyone sit down on an invisible chair?"

Melba nodded. "Usually there's a wall, though," she said. "You pretend the wall is a chair and sit down. It engages the quadriceps."

"He's up again," said Don Pond. "Shadow boxing."

"I suppose the bakery hasn't warmed the street any," said Melba. "He must be freezing in just that light coat and fringe of hair. But why is he there?"

"He's making sure I convince you to come with me," said Don Pond.

"My leaving the bakery was Dr. Buck's idea?" gasped Melba. "When you said the men in this town . . ."

"You didn't know I meant Dr. Buck?" Don Pond's voice was frankly incredulous. "You think the laypeople of Dan have gotten into the habit of diagnosing safe and unsafe without the help of a doctor? Melba, Dr. Buck is the only person in this town qualified to make decisions about your wellbeing. He told me you have a condition that makes you mistrustful of representatives of the medical profession and that you'd be more likely to heed my advice if I pretended it came from a group of anonymous men, men who'd reached their decision through a democratic process. I was under no circumstance to reveal Dr. Buck's leading role in the matter. Now I've blown it," Don Pond sighed. "But why can't you obey Dr. Buck, like the rest of us? He's not a small man, and his hands aren't too cold or too hot. Before Dr. Buck, you wouldn't remember, but Dr. Clamp doctored in Dan, and he had a mystifying head of hair. What's more, he was never the right temperature! How can you give yourself freely to a doctor who isn't the right temperature? What's more elementary than temperature? Even the smallest doctor in the world knows how to regulate temperature. Dr. Buck got rid of Dr. Clamp easily enough . . ."

"Was there a funeral?" asked Melba. "I do seem to remember the town hall filled with casseroles, all different kinds, spaghetti, creamed corn, turkey divine, queasy tuna, mushroom potpourri, the one that's made of five different congealed soups . . ."

"Five soup casserole," murmured Don Pond.

"Five soup casserole, oyster cheese casserole . . . that was a funeral, wasn't it?"

"Sure it was," said Don Pond. Around his beard, the face had paled in patches and purpled in others. His words came slowly. Don Pond's head was very small, and so usually words seemed to issue forth rapidly in a high thin stream. But these words were dark and thick, sluggishly emitted.

"But Melba," said Don Pond, and the words and the movements of his mouth were misaligned, the words filling the air like sludge and the mouth stretching out and folding in again, so that Melba's head jerked back and forth, following first the trajectory of the words then the ponderous motions of the mouth.

"It . . ." said Don Pond, "wasn't . . ."

Melba's hands clasped together.

"Dr. Clamp's funeral . . ." said Don Pond.

"Then whose . . ." Melba began, but her world was going dark. She felt as she did when, like Ned Hat, she had been driven by circumstances to fill her mouth with hydrogen peroxide. She would drink the peroxide swishingly and grip the edge of the sink as her gums began to seethe. In those moments, her roaring mouth sounded like the inside of a conch shell, which sounded, in turn, like the outside of the ocean, and through these echoes—a form of geo-sonar—Melba felt that she could establish, briefly, a sense of her location on the earth. She could also establish other things. For example, her body had the consistency of a stone fruit, although with a different ratio of hard parts to soft parts, and those parts differently distributed. She had a keen sense of the human body—blemished and juicy, a lobe of oddly shaped flesh clinging to an oddly shaped pit—and of Dan, the endless thicket in which these bodies formed, growing in clusters but dropping one by one to rot in the understory, contributing nurturing ooze to the tangle of brambles and brackens ever-spreading their roots.

The word "bracken" shot through Melba's mind. She swayed.

"Samovar . . ." She murmured the word just as "bracken" banged into it. She saw a spark that began to ripple and then she knew no more.

When Melba awoke she was no longer in the bakery. She was inside a small house, darkly paneled. She was stretched out on a long hard sofa with very wide armrests.

"I was having a dream!" she said, starting up. Everywhere, there had been buildings, but irregular buildings, with too few or too many walls. She had walked through the rooms and in room after room, curtains or vines or racks of meat hung down from the ceilings, but finally she had entered a room with a ceiling from which nothing hung down. The ceiling was made of clouds and through the breaks in the ceiling clouds she could see the clouds of the real sky above them.

"I think the moon had gone missing?" Melba said. "And I was looking for it?" Melba looked at the ceiling. It was white and bumpy, with a protuberant light fixture she did not care for.

"Drink this." Someone was pushing a mug into her hand and Melba clutched it. The mug had no handle. The mug was so heavily made, however, that the outside was warmed only slightly by the steaming liquid in the central well. Melba held it gratefully with two hands.

"Coffee," murmured Melba, lowering her face to the mug. She blinked away the steam, wiggling on the couch. The couch was nearly as deep as it was long. Unless Melba sat on the edge of a cushion her feet did not touch the ground. The black vinyl squeaked as she scooted forward and she heard a low indulgent chuckle.

"Do I hear Melba's little otter?"

Melba blinked harder but sleep and steam clung to her eyeballs.

"Who's there?" she asked.

"Don Pond, Melba," came the answer, and as Melba blinked she focused at last on Don Pond's small head. The size of the head and the uneven complexion reminded Melba of a gourd, and she smiled, reassured. Gourds, useless in themselves, are displayed to indicate hominess and abundance, and Melba was not impervious to the signification.

"Don Pond," she sighed. "So this is your house!" In addition to the enormous couch, she now made out a few other features of Don Pond's house: a low coffee table parallel to the couch and, on the other side, a loveseat on which Don Pond sat comfortably. Don Pond had removed his shoes and socks and his bare feet were nestled in the thick mustard-colored carpet. Melba wiggled her toes, realizing that her own shoes had been removed. In the paneled wall behind Don Pond, two windows filtered the daylight, but, as filters, the windows were not fine; the daylight that entered the room could not even be considered granular; it was chunky, practically obscured by impurities. Melba tried not to purse her lips or demonstrate her superiority in any way.

"I never realized how close your house really is to the bakery," said Melba, to make conversation. "I only shut my eyes for a moment and here I am! I'm surprised I haven't ended up here before, by accident. I rush about in the bakery, and I can imagine tripping over a broom and suddenly getting flung directly onto this couch. I suppose that's near enough to what happened."

She lowered her face again to the mug and sniffed.

"Why Don, this isn't coffee . . ." she trailed off.

"Of course it's not," said Don Pond. "You've never known me to serve coffee, and I wouldn't start now, when my main goal is to put you at your ease, to keep everything nice and normal. I find coffee off-putting and viscous."

"Hmmm," Melba swung her legs, snuffling at the mug, working the scent up her nostrils as she tried to identify the components. She couldn't distract herself, though, from Don Pond's ill-considered remark and, sighing, realized that she had to contradict him.

"I can't agree with you, Don," said Melba. "Not about coffee. I know I'm being quarrelsome. But wouldn't you describe coffee differently if you considered longer? Imagine you're taking a sip of coffee. Now hold the coffee in your mouth. Don't you find it different than what you described? It's not off-putting and viscous, is it? Why it's soothing," exclaimed Melba. "Soothing and jarring. That's exactly what coffee is. Rather complex, but I'm sure you can tell if you concentrate."

Melba wished she could brew Don Pond her special coffee, in case his imagination had flaws. Her coffee had been tested again and again, and she knew for certain that it always produced exactly those effects. To be soothed but also jarred—this was what Melba most needed, and that was what coffee, all coffee, but Melba's coffee above all others, delivered. Randal Hans had said he needed this too. But perhaps Randal Hans had only said this to be confirming, because when he was Melba's boyfriend, he exerted himself, verbally, to confirm many of her statements, which he later negated in writing.

The circumference of Don Pond's beard contracted slightly. He was pursing his mouth, concentrating on the imaginary mouthful. Then he shook his head.

"No," he said. "I'm really put off. There's a gluey, bitter taint to my saliva now. No, I don't like it."

Melba averted her eyes. Apparently Don Pond was not her boyfriend, or at least not the confirming kind. Melba smiled a little to herself. She didn't want Don Pond for a boyfriend anyway. She liked his head more and more, but other than his head he did not have a great deal to recommend him. He did not need to be soothed and jarred for one thing, or, at least, not by coffee. Perhaps he was soothed and jarred by something else? A pet?

Melba had noticed that people with pets sometimes put less emphasis on coffee than people without pets. Pets, she suspected, performed a service similar to coffee. Pets were always bounding onto their owners' beds in the mornings, tonguing and clawing and defecating and yelping joyously.

Yes, it amounted to the same thing, thought Melba. Did Don Pond keep pets? She cocked her head, listening. She heard noises coming from the corners of the house, but the noises didn't prove the presence of pets. Melba Zuzzo's house was filled with noises, chirps, hisses, grunts, scratchings, and scrabblings, but she didn't call the animals who made these noises *pets*. They didn't bound for one thing, but scurried, and their behavior was sly and unredeemed. Those animals were not carefree like pets, and they displayed none of the pet's easy sovereignty.

Don Pond gestured at the coffee table on which Melba noted a thick book, a wooden yo-yo, a teapot, an oilcan, and several garlic sticks laid in a row on top of the bakery bag. Melba felt herself flush as she caught sight of the garlic crumbs smattering the highly glossed surface of the table. So Don Pond hadn't forgotten.

"I prefer tea to coffee," said Don Pond. "This tea I've steeped for you is anti-viral, with tumor-inhibiting properties."

Melba clapped a hand to her earlobe. The carbuncle had grown. It was a tumor? She searched Don Pond's face. She read nothing there, but the insinuating thrust of his words could not be parried. She probed the ear, probed it again. A tumor. She should have known.

"Who told you about the tumor?" she demanded.

"No one had to tell me," said Don Pond. "I'm not blind. But Dr. Buck isn't calling it a death sentence. He says that you haven't assumed leadership of your family, that you aren't ready for a serious illness."

"That's true of Melba Zuzzo," whispered Melba. "But if there's any truth to the allegations . . . Don, Ned Hat has alleged . . ."

"Dammit, Melba, nobody believes the allegations." Don Pond

tossed his head, and stroked his beard up and down, fingers hooked into claws.

"Oh!" Breathing hard, Melba set her mug carefully beside her on the cushion and launched herself from the couch, hitting the carpet on all fours. She stood up shakily, bumping the coffee table with her shin.

"I need to pace, Don," she said. Don Pond nodded. He had calmed considerably.

"That's fine, Melba," he said.

"I'll be careful I don't end up at the bakery!" She gave Don a watery smile and in response a smile opened in the beard, splitting the gourdlike head. Melba circled the coffee table warily. It was very close to both the couch and the loveseat and as she paced the length of the table on either side her legs brushed alternately the couch and the legs of Don Pond.

"Let me put on some music," said Don Pond, tactfully. He stood and disappeared into the corner of the house. The house was not big, but Don Pond matched the house very closely, and he was difficult to see as he bent and fiddled.

"This music was recorded in a cave," he called. "If you don't like it, I can play something else."

"I'm sure it's fine," said Melba.

"I bet it'd be something special to listen to it, also in a cave," said Don Pond, returning to the loveseat.

"It sounds like fluttering," said Melba.

"That's right!" said Don Pond. "There's fluttering, and it's very dark, and you're in the company of personified forces."

Melba's legs brushed Don Pond's legs as she squeezed between the loveseat and the table. She tried to hurry her pacing, but her skirts and apron tangled her up and she fell, turning her body sideways so that she landed in the slot between the chair and the table, upsetting neither. It was skillfully done.

"Oh don't move," said Melba, because she could feel Don Pond shifting his weight. "I'm going to lie here for just a moment." The thick carpet cushioned the side of her face and if she angled up her eyes she could see the legs and the underside of the table, less highly glossed than the surface. Her ribs pressed protuberances—Don Pond's feet—and her back pressed against Don Pond's legs. Suddenly, she recalled, in vivid detail, a holiday. She had spent the holiday with Randal Hans, the two of them in dungarees, riding the same bike. After many hours, they dismounted, ate string cheese, and laughed about Melampus, who had announced to Melba the day before that she had decided to succeed Ann Dump as town clerk.

"But Ann Dump is so young!" laughed Randal Hans. "Younger than Melampus, and she would never give up her position. Ann Dump told me she was born to be the town clerk and that she would die as town clerk, and Ann Dump should know! She controls all the records in Dan. Melampus is very determined, and she is very beautiful and unafraid of hard work, but that will only set Ann

Dump more firmly against her. Doesn't Melampus wonder why she is named after a snail? Doesn't she remember that she used to be named something else, something more appropriate for a beautiful girl? Who does she think changed her name to Melampus?"

Melba was laughing too hard to answer. Her mouth tasted mild and grassy with the string cheese and she was so happy!

"Melampus is stubborn and foolish!" she sputtered at last. "She says she likes the name Melampus. She says Ann Dump's changing her name can only be considered a mark of distinction. She says only termagants and other women without desirable qualities prefer the names they were given at birth to the names they might acquire later on, through another person's discretion. She even says she likes snails!"

Randal Hans's eyes had disappeared; his cheeks were swollen with laughter. Melba grasped Randal Hans's right hand.

"What do you most want in the world?" Melba asked Randal Hans, impulsively. Randal Hans hiccupped, then giggled, then drew a long breath, wiping his eyes which were just beginning to reemerge.

"I would like to be town clerk!" he screamed, doubling over. When he and Melba caught their breath again, he unwrapped a piece of string cheese and nibbled it, more or less soberly. He seemed to be thinking. They were at the top of Jake Hill so Randal Hans could look down at Dan as he thought. Lop Street and Satin Street and

Hotot Street and White Street and Dwarf Street and Spot Street and Wooly Street and Tan Street and Main Street and Champagne D'Argent Avenue—all below, crisscrossing or winding off, missing the other streets completely, dead-ending in some lot or field, visible at this height as a pale or sable patch. Randal Hans had propped the bike against a telephone pole and he and Melba sat down beside it on a flattened box.

"I would like to be ribbon-shaped," said Randal Hans at last.

"But not a ribbon?" said Melba Zuzzo cautiously, afraid of ruining the moment.

"Not a ribbon," said Randal Hans. "A flatworm, maybe. Something that wiggles into the mud and the mud exerts even pressure on every part of its body."

"You want to be squeezed?" offered Melba Zuzzo, more cautiously still. She bit into her string cheese, then, emboldened, flung the remainder into the dark tangle of roadside vines. She cupped her mouth with her hand. Her hand smelled sweeter than the string cheese. It smelled like a prune. She swayed toward Randal Hans and their shoulders jolted together.

"I want to be squeezed evenly," said Randal Hans. "All over. It wouldn't be possible from a human." He sounded wistful.

"A bear?" asked Melba Zuzzo.

"It would have to be four bears," said Randal Hans. "Enough to make a cube, or a sphere." He continued to stare at Dan, the rooftops and scaly greenery and the sluggish holiday foot traffic, and Melba stared at Randal Hans. His yellow hair had picked up a stain, as though he'd been wearing a freshly dyed borsalino. Melba imagined squeezing Randal Hans, squeezing him tightly, joining forces with three bears, all of them working together, finding some way to exert synchronous pressures, wrapping Randal Hans in fur and flesh and bone, the bears blowing hot, fishy air from their mouths on her face and neck. She wouldn't like that one bit. But if it was what Randal Hans wanted most . . .

"I'll do it," said Melba, but Randal Hans was pointing past her, at a gray spot on the edge of Dan, and didn't pay her any mind.

"Look there," said Randal Hans. "Did those kids just dig up a body in the gravel pit?" Melba looked and shrugged.

"Are they kids?" she asked. "Or could they be badgers? They're so far away who could tell? But something about the way they dig, their determination . . . It's obvious they know what they're doing and that nobody's whining about it."

"You must be right," said Randal Hans. He held up his empty hands and smiled at Melba. "No more cheese! Let's get out of here."

Then he and Melba had pushed the bike over the summit of Jake Hill. There was no street on the other side, just weeds interspersed with morasses and trash. They hopped across a stinking rivulet to a place Randal Hans remembered where people dumped batteries.

Now, lying on Don Pond's floor, in that narrow space between the chair and the carpet and the table, molded to Don Pond's legs and feet, Melba felt that she understood Randal Hans, his craving, not for bears or mud in particular, but for an all-encompassing proximity. She felt that she belonged where she lay, with Don Pond and the chair and carpet and the table close around her. Her relationship with Don Pon was different now that they weren't in the bakery. Now that she knew how she fit into his house, nothing could be like it was before.

"I know what you're doing," said Don Pond. "You're making a cave, aren't you? I've done the same thing. I've even written up proclamations for my cave, seceding from Dan."

"Don't talk," begged Melba, her voice muffled. "You're spoiling it."

"Well, I can't see how I'm spoiling anything," said Don Pond, stiffly. "I know you're using me as part of your cave. Dr. Buck warned me about letting you do exactly this, about letting you use me in this way. He said you have a kind of bleak power over people, that you turn men into stalagmites, but you don't stay with them for long. You break into a stream of bats and rush away."

"Is that what he said?" whispered Melba.

"Not exactly," said Don Pond. "How could I say what Dr. Buck said? I'm not a doctor. It's an approximation, Melba." Don Pond's toes jabbed between Melba's ribs as he struggled up. Melba heard him stumbling through the house and fiddling with knobs and all at once the fluttering music died away. Melba crawled out from her slot. She felt dizzy and stumbled around the coffee table, climbing back onto the couch. Don Pond was standing at one end of the couch, looking at her.

"I'm not a doctor," he said. "I'm not even a patient. I was the first customer at the bakery, but I gave that up for you."

"How's that?" asked Melba.

"Where are you, Melba?" said Don Pond, throwing out his arms. "You can't claim that this is the bakery."

"It's your house, I know," said Melba Zuzzo. "But really, it could be somewhere inside the bakery. The bakery is enormous and I never go past the first mixer or deep into the freezer. For all I know, your house might be inside the freezer. It's warm enough in here, but who knows what it's like once you open the door? No, I wouldn't be surprised if we were still in the bakery. I always thought you had an arrangement with Leslie Duck."

"He's my landlord," said Don Pond. "But that doesn't mean my house is inside the bakery. Landlords own multiple properties, often non-contiguous. And if my house is in fact separate from the bakery, which it is, and you are in my house, which you are, then you are not in the bakery. The bakery, Melba, is effectively closed for business."

Melba saw what he was getting at and tried to wave him off but he would not be silenced.

"How can I be the first customer, Melba, if there are no subsequent customers?" asked Don Pond. "By removing you from the bakery, I sacrificed my only defining characteristic and my only hope of compelling respect from other people. Not that being the first customer was a skill I developed on my own," Don Pond added, modestly, in a manner that recalled his former self. "As you pointed out, I owed it to Leslie Duck, who rented me this property. But I like to think I went above and beyond the bare minimum required of a first customer."

"You did," Melba agreed. "The garlic . . ."

Don Pond leaned across the armrest. It was longer than Don Pond's torso and so he ended up splayed across it on his belly in a seal-like posture.

"You noticed!" he said. "You cared."

Melba fumbled for some way of expressing what Don Pond had meant to her. "First customer" didn't seem adequate, but how else could she describe the role he played in her life? She slid away from him toward the other end of the couch, chewing the collar of her shirt.

"Your head," she said, releasing the collar, using her fingertips to press the damp wrinkles against her neck. "You probably think I'm indifferent to it, but you're wrong. I feel tense and distracted. It's as if your head were a hard ball balanced on a seal's nose and the seal might toss it to me, but Don, what if I miss?"

Don Pond groaned. The couch seemed to get longer by the second and Don Pond's groan came from far off.

"Melba, you wouldn't miss," he groaned. "Not if you didn't want to. You know you can just hold up the ends of your apron and catch anything. But it's no good trying to convince you. You aren't compassionate. You lorded it over everyone when you worked at the bakery. Now that that's over, I wonder what you'll do? In a way, you've lost more than I have."

Melba did not know how to respond. It was too new, leaving her position at the bakery, the bakery closing for business, the day stretching out before her without activities or tasks. Curled in the corner of the couch, she contemplated the black vinyl expanse. The couch was really a showpiece, one of a kind, grimly magnificent, the house merely a shanty built over the couch to protect it from the elements. The cold, claylike cushions cased in the thin, vaguely tacky membrane—they did give one the sensation of snuggling dead flesh. Even the faint chemical odor of the couch seemed preservative in nature. Melba rubbed her hand on the vinyl and examined the pad of her thumb—no darker, but waxier.

Summoning all her strength, Melba crawled from the couch corner toward what she hoped was the cushion's edge, a matte black horizon line where the gleaming vinyl graded into the dim and porous air. The vista dizzied her. She swung her arm, using the momentum to propel herself backwards away from the edge. She bumped against her abandoned mug and the tea sloshed but did not spill. She fumbled for it, grasping the mug in both hands and gulping without hesitation. The taste was not good. The texture, however, reminded Melba pleasantly of silt.

Like any female in a male's house, she thought, I am being struck with ways to make improvements. She smiled, relieved to find that she had surrendered her contested singularity and merged herself with the anonymous multitude of women in general.

For instance, thought Melba, improvingly, enjoying her new-found freedom as representative of a group, how nice it would be to serve such a tea in a small dish, just the slightest bit concave! The silty tea would spread out wide and warm and shallow, and the guest could drink it with eyes fixed on the brown surface, as though peeping through rushes at the squidgy rim of a eutrophic lake. Having seen her improving idea to the finish, Melba sighed, her mind returning to its lonely track.

She heard rummaging and clinking and wondered briefly if animals had emerged from wallows beneath the couch before she glimpsed Don Pond setting a platter on the coffee table. The platter was rectangular, white plastic, arrayed with daubs of jam and sliced sausages in alternating lines. Melba noted the thin, curved shadow limning the blade of a white plastic knife. Setting her mug beside her on the cushion, she squirmed to the edge of the couch and extended her arm across the crevasse between couch and table until her hand hovered above the tabletop. After making a few calculations, she let her hand drop onto the platter and pinched with thumb and forefinger, coming away with a firm grip on the knife's handle. She performed a similar maneuver and a garlic stick was also hers. She reached out the other arm and spread jam on the garlic stick. The jam clung together in a dense clot that fell from the end of the garlic stick and was lost to view, tumbling down to be swallowed by the carpet. Don Pond did not glance over. He was ignoring her, had crossed to the other side of the room, where he stood cleaning the windowsills with a hand vacuum.

Engaging her back muscles, Melba retracted her arms, regaining her position on the edge of the couch with her prizes in her hands. She sniffed the jam, which smelled gamey, then crunched the garlic stick between her teeth. Don Pond switched off the hand vacuum and she froze, jaws clenched, the garlic stick lodged in her mouth. The hand vacuum surged to life and Melba blew out through her nose, a noisy gust of air, and mauled the garlic stick with powerful up and down and also lateral motions of her jaws, snorting, the garlic stick itself grown wet and pliable, folding silently now into a sodden but lacy ball. She swallowed, blew again through her nose, and let herself be pulled backwards by the couch's inexorable gravity. Soon she was back in the corner.

So this was what it is like to be unemployed, thought Melba. Navigating a man's couch, poaching in the thick unclean daylight, as the man bustles about, hosting.

Of course, Melba knew there were different forms of unemployment; some people opted for chemical comas, others ate pears in the face of the wind that blew strongly on the top of the mountain, others shopped, relying on the television and telephone to identify goods and place orders, or visiting the outlet stores on White Street where damaged or slightly soiled blouses and slacks appeared in bins at unpredictable intervals. Melba Zuzzo did not shop very often, never having had the time, but some girls shopped a great deal.

Melba had been warned by her mother that she did not shop enough, and that by not shopping enough she was jeopardizing her chances for long-term happiness. The conversation had shocked her, but whether it was because of what her mother had said, or because she had not expected to speak to her mother at all on that occasion, she could not be sure. She had picked up the telephone to place a call to Mark Rand.

"Mark Rand?" she had said.

"Speaking," replied Gigi Zuzzo.

Melba had paused, perplexed. She had felt the impulse to pull the telephone receiver from her head and examine it, but she did not give in to this impulse, which she knew to be a stupid one. Instead she looked around the vestibule, where her coats hung on pegs and the telephone sat in the center of a tiny telephone table.

"Do you want to know what he's saying?" asked Gigi Zuzzo. Melba heard muffled laughter.

"Yes," said Melba.

"Melba!" barked Gigi Zuzzo. "Did you really mean to call a man, a landlord, at his private residence, so as to demand a report on what he is at that moment saying in a private conversation with a female visitor?"

"No," said Melba. "That is . . ."

"Good," said Gigi Zuzzo. "It would reflect badly on me. It would embarrass me in front of a landlord, and Mark Rand and I have just gotten past all of that, our differences in status."

"There's a fume," said Melba Zuzzo. "In the house."

"I should hope it's in the house if you're calling Mark Rand," said Gigi Zuzzo. "A landlord has a great deal of responsibility, it's true, but he can't be expected to go about looking into every stray fume that attracts a tenant's notice. Have you heard of the atmosphere?"

"Yes," said Melba. "But . . ."

"Well that's the source of fumes, Melba. Now do you think it's Mark Rand's job to upkeep the atmosphere?"

"No," said Melba. "I . . ."

"Whose job is it?" asked Gigi Zuzzo.

"Astronauts?" guessed Melba. She heard a faint pop.

"Did you hear that?" asked Gigi Zuzzo. "I snapped my fingers! Yes, Melba. Astronauts. The division of labor gives us landlords and astronauts, thank goodness, or men like Mark Rand would never rest. He's overworked as it is. You don't understand what it's like. Mark Rand does rest, make no mistake, but rarely. He has a bed for nodding off now and then, but it's impossible for him to spend an entire night in his bed. For one thing, many people use it and not all of them use it at the same time. You sign up for particular timeslots and pay accordingly. Mark Rand is a landlord in the first instance, so even if he is so tired he's swaying on his feet, he would never do anything irregular. He would never evict the people in his bed without the proper notice, and by the time he gave the people proper notice, they would be out of the bed anyway, and new people in their stead. Now why would you bother Mark Rand when, for practical and ethical purposes, an astronaut is the appropriate choice?"

Melba considered. Like most people, in the course of her life she had come into contact with an astronaut, but only briefly, in a controlled setting, and she had no idea where he might be now. Of all people, astronauts can be in the most places—anywhere on earth, but also anywhere not on earth—and so it is especially difficult to guess their location. Melba tried to summon a picture of the astronaut as she had seen him in the auditorium and later the cafeteria of Dan Elementary. It was so long ago! Had he worn a powder blue tunic and white boots? She thought that he had.

In the auditorium, he had stood before the gathered students with Principal Benjamin. After the cheering died away, Principal Benjamin had spoken, not into a microphone, but into an intercom, so that his voice boomed from above, both in the auditorium and in the empty classrooms, perhaps for the benefit of the terrariums. Melba remembered that he had spoken on the topic of color—color, according to certain professionals, is not a part of things, not even things known chiefly for their colors, flowers and tropical birds and the most delicious of the cartoon-themed boxed cereals, but rather color gets attached to their surfaces later on, and Principal Benjamin must have had plenty to say about when and how the colors are attached, and Melba felt certain she had asked perspicacious questions about methods used to detach the colors and whether or not the detached colors could be stored, and if they were scented or had particular tastes, which seemed likely based on everyone's experience, for example, of red—but as she devoted more energy to remembering and began to hear the voice transmitting over the intercom, she discovered that the words did not bear out her initial thought that Principal Benjamin had spoken about color, unless of course he had spoken in code, which was not impossible. No, the more Melba thought, the more she remembered that he had not spoken on the topic of color. She could hear his voice as he spoke on another topic altogether:

"Force and motion, my buckaroos, there's no escape," boomed Principal Benjamin. "Surrender your illusions. No one floats, not even in space. Astronauts are falling! Does this make you sad? It shouldn't. Are you cowboys or tintypes? Wake up! Die on the ground, with your boots on. Do you have goldfish?"

"Yes!" called Melba. She was sitting in the front row and Principal Benjamin pointed a finger at her, nodding gravely, before going on.

"Is the bowl spotless, suffused with radiant energy? Is there a light shining in the castle window? Do you change the water? Do you keep fewer than two-inches of fish per gallon?"

"The fish don't stay still," said Melba. "I think—"

"Or is there slime on the bowl?" said Principal Benjamin. "Are the castle walls over-grown? Is there everywhere darkness and filth?

Are there sheets of living tissue in the water? What if you purchased an algae-eating fish? Have you considered it?"

"Yes," whispered Melba.

"Yes!" crowed Principal Benjamin. "Of course you have. Who hasn't? Imagine this algae-eater. You're holding it up in a small plastic bag. It's skinny. It's hungry. Now let it go. Drop it in the bowl. Let it feast. Let it begin by devouring the proteinaceous film on the surface of the water. Let it move on to the slime on the walls. Below, every rock has a beard. So much shag, so much sludge. What a smorgasbord! Do you think your algae-eater can swallow all that muck, all that gunk, all that fuzz? Do the hairs tickle its throat? Does it gag?"

Melba held her breath. She felt, in her own throat, a tickle. She shook her head. Her eyes watered. Principal Benjamin's eyes were watering too.

"No!" he cried. "It explodes! It explodes into bits and every bit needs to eat. Every bit eats until it explodes. Don't you see? There are infinite bits exploding infinite times until there's nothing else left to eat. The biosphere is all bits eating bits! We're all done. We're all ooze. I'm sure our guest, Mr. Gray, would tell you as much, if I hadn't exhausted the subject. And now let us adjourn to the cafeteria. Thank you."

Melba had joined the flow of children out of the auditorium and through a tiled corridor where she waited in line to scrub her hands at a long trough before walking on, filing with the others through the cafeteria doors, each child pausing before Nurse Nathan to receive a spoonful of dark paste doled from a colossal jar. Melba swallowed her paste, scanning the cafeteria tables. The astronaut, she saw, was in the middle of the room, seated across from Principal Benjamin at Principal Benjamin's desk, which Lester Crane, the custodian, had carried into the cafeteria for the occasion. Melba hovered near the desk anxiously, but Principal Benjamin and Mr. Gray were studying their trays and did not acknowledge her. She stepped closer to Mr. Gray and noted that his tunic smelled of ozone. She opened her mouth to speak. Suddenly, she felt a hand clap down on the back of her neck and she was steered away from the desk, reprimanded harshly, and sent to the Principal's office, where she cried a little, cross-legged on one of the clean squares of linoleum formerly concealed by Principal Benjamin's desk.

Try as she might, Melba could not recall what happened next. When she attempted to reconstruct the sequence, her mind jumped from the image of the barren office to an image of the area below her kitchen sink, dark and cluttered with pipes, pale bottles, and a tall, dented box, one corner savaged and spilling blue powder. Principal Benjamin's office and the area below her kitchen sink, envisioned one after the other, did make a kind of sequence, but not the sequence Melba wanted. That is, they didn't make a linear sequence, but rather an associative sequence, which perhaps told her something about her consciousness but told her less than nothing about the order in which the events in her life unfolded. But was there an order? And if so, was that order chronological? And if so, chronological in which direction? Melba knew these weren't fit questions for a landlord, but could they be considered fit questions for an astronaut?

Well, thought Melba, no use wondering. Only Principal Benjamin might have had some insight into Mr. Gray's whereabouts, and Principal Benjamin had disappeared. Melba had no way to contact an astronaut on her own.

"I do not have the telephone number for any astronaut," replied Melba, primly.

"I do not have the telephone number for any astronaut," mimicked Gigi Zuzzo. "So Mark Rand must receive every telephone call intended for a person whose number you do not have? How many telephone numbers don't you have? Why it's an unconceivable amount. Boggling. Do you see what kind of burden you place on Mark Rand? Even a landlord of his caliber couldn't bear up under it, and that's supposing you were his only tenant, which you are not."

"I didn't mean," began Melba, but Gigi Zuzzo cut her off.

"Of course, you didn't mean," said Gigi Zuzzo. "You never mean anything. You never anticipate, Melba. You don't understand the concept of the future. What's the future? Tell me."

"What if I don't tell you?" asked Melba desperately. "Will it just happen?"

Gigi Zuzzo growled long and low, and Melba clung to the phone, sweat breaking out along her brow.

"Does the future have something to do with snow?" she asked. "How it doesn't fall from the sky all at once, crushing everything below?"

"You're just like your father," said Gigi Zuzzo bitterly. "You always think things are so much rosier than they really are. Let me tell you, the future never kept anyone from getting crushed! I've noticed that you never buy depilatory creams, Melba. Your arms are fuzzy, don't deny it, matted with little hairs, like tennis balls. Now listen to this. One day you're going to see something startling and not in a good way. You'll see a piece of straw driven like a skewer through a man's neck by gale force winds. How awful! Who wants to see such a thing? Not you! You'll throw your arm across your eyes and those little hairs will act like Velcro on your eyeballs. You'll rip out your eyeballs. They'll be stuck to your arm! That's the future, Melba. That's what not meaning gets you, eyeballs on your arm. Why won't you buy depilatory creams? They smell wonderful, like scorched lemons. They're cheap! You never shop, Melba. It's killing you, not just in the future, right now."

"I had a bad experience with depilatory creams," said Melba. "My skin started to smoke, the skin above my upper lip, and the smoke went right into my nose. I had to wear your snorkel and sleep with my face in a bowl of water. I couldn't possibly go through that again! I don't even have my own snorkel, and . . ."

"It's not about the depilatory creams," said Gigi Zuzzo. "It's about shopping more generally. When you shop, you expand, Melba. You stretch out your hand and also your psyche to compass the thing that you desire, and then, when the moment is right, you clamp down, you squeeze around the thing! Expansion and contraction, Melba, that's shopping. It's a spasm! A special spasm. You've heard of these spasms? Not just a pleasant jolt. Jolts don't penetrate to great depth, and they have no duration. A spasm is different; it's a rippling that works the fascia to keep your inner linings from drying out. Have you ever seen a person with her inner linings dried out?"

Melba considered.

"You have," snarled Gigi Zuzzo. "Think, Melba. She never shopped! She worked in the bakery before you. How can you be so callous? You are her successor!"

"Lisa Cucci," said Melba. She had succeeded Lisa Cucci as the bakery's employee.

"But Lisa Cucci's inner lining didn't dry out," protested Melba. "She married Seton Holmes and started a new life."

"Lisa Cucci was spurned by Seton Holmes!" said Gigi Zuzzo. "The Business Council decided that the story should be suppressed. They kept it from you, Melba. I disagreed, but I'm not on the Business Council. I had no vote. What do I know about business? Nothing. If you'd been informed about Lisa Cucci's being dried out and spurned, a husk of her former self, you might not have performed ably as her successor. You might have feared acceding to her position, knowing how it turned out. In that sense, I see the wisdom of the Business Council's decision. In another sense though, I see the fallibility of the Business Council's reasoning, because in not knowing Lisa Cucci's situation, you have made almost exactly the same mistakes. It doesn't bode well for your longevity as a bakery employee! But I suppose the Business Council made calculations about all of that, about your rate of deterioration under Lisa Cucci-like conditions. They are already training your successor!"

"If Lisa Cucci didn't start a new life with Seton Holmes," whispered Melba. "And she isn't living her old life as a bakery employee, then what is Lisa Cucci doing?"

"She's existing in a kind of limbo," said Gigi Zuzzo. "She doesn't *do* anything. She can't. She's neither here nor there, this nor that. You wouldn't recognize her. She's a wispy, pale thing, a tuft. It's as though she's been reduced to a single eyebrow. I bid you good day, Melba."

"Good day," said Melba.

"You don't raise me?" snapped Gigi Zuzzo. "You see my bid and that's all? Melba, have you no loins? No spark? Don't you aspire?"

"I don't think so," said Melba.

"Good day," said Gigi Zuzzo.

"Good day," said Melba.

"Don," called Melba now over the moan of the hand vacuum. "Don." Don whirled, hand vacuum pointed at Melba's head. For an instant, Don Pond and Melba Zuzzo stared at each other, Melba's eyes flitting between Don Pond's eyes and the dark slot of the upraised hand vacuum. Then Don Pond lowered the hand vacuum.

"Yes, Melba," he said.

"Do you notice anything about my eyebrows?" asked Melba. "I mean, do you recognize anyone?"

Don Pond shrugged.

"Dr. Buck warned me you would ask about that," he said. "He told me that you would become agitated whatever answer I gave and so I shouldn't say anything. He recommended that I assign you to a part of the house where your mind would be occupied by a form of entertainment."

"I'll go," said Melba. "I've heard that entertainment is a cure for being tired and for being wide awake as well. It might be exactly what I need. I didn't know there was any part of Dan with a functioning form of entertainment."

"You haven't been paying much attention to the candidates if you think they're making promises about entertainment," said Don Pond. "Haven't you been listening to the speeches?"

"Only when I can't avoid them," said Melba. "When someone calls me at the bakery or at my house or bikes along next to me with a megaphone."

"I like that you look at my head when you talk to me," said Don Pond in a rush. "Dr. Buck told me not to say that to you either, but I couldn't help it."

"Thank you," said Melba, looking at Don Pond's head more intently, although she knew that she did not deserve his compliment. As a girl, she hadn't given heads their due, until one day her father took her to the Dan Diner. There she was reprimanded by the waitress, Barb Owen. Barb Owen had slammed mugs of coffee on the table, jostling the pink tablet settling into Melba's drinking water. Melba stared at the bubbles streaming up inside the tall glass of drinking water. She skimmed the surface foam with the tip of her spoon then placed the spoon carefully on the napkin beside two other spoons. She wondered what to order. She thought she might like something with gravy. Meanwhile, Zeno Zuzzo was talking about the landbridge.

"In conclusion, crossing the landbridge was a beleaguering experience," concluded Zeno Zuzzo. "I would have swum! But land was the new thing then. It was like a fad! Walking on land was the big thing."

"Were there shoes yet?" asked Melba.

"No shoes," said Zeno Zuzzo. He ordered the lunch special and Barb Owen brought Zeno and Melba Zuzzo each a Turkey Dinner. She slammed them on the table. Melba watched the gravy slowly lap the rim of the gravy boat. After finishing her Turkey Dinner, Melba waited at the door while her father brought the check up to the counter. Suddenly Barb Owen was beside her, bending over her, pushing her face close to Melba's face.

"You are an anarchist, Melba Zuzzo," she shouted. "You're always looking at people's hands or talking about their feet! Why can't you pay attention to heads like a regular person?"

Stunned, Melba shrank back, but not before she had looked closely at Barb Owen's head. She understood in an instant why Barb

Owen was upset. Barb Owen had a sensational head, a head that warranted inspection. Melba had never thought of herself as an anarchist, but whatever term you put to it, her behavior had been wrong: looking down all the time, introducing shoes into conversation while sitting down at the table to eat turkey and gravy in a public venue. If it wasn't anarchism, it was something very close, and Melba felt deeply ashamed, a feeling that stayed with her no matter how much praise she received. It felt good, receiving praise from Don Pond, but it could not alleviate the shame. Barb Owen deserved the praise, not Melba. Melba's smile was bittersweet.

"Anyway," she said, "I don't care very much about politics. Mayor Bunt is as good a mayor as any other, so why we have to go through an election is beyond me."

"I know someone who might change your mind," said Don Pond. "He's a candidate and if he wins the election he's going to transform Dan completely."

"Is that what you want?" asked Melba, curious.

"Depends on the kind of transformation," said Don Pond. "This candidate will make us all rich. I don't care so much about being rich myself, but it would be nice to be a citizen in a town of millionaires. Everyone in Henderson would go green with envy and everyone in Gerardville and Manstown and Wilma too, everyone in every town everywhere, once they hear how high on the hog we all are. We'll have to fill all the warehouses in the hosiery district with our riches. I don't know if you've noticed Melba, ensconced in the bakery like you are, but there's a dearth of jobs in Dan. Unemployment is more enjoyable if you're rich and this candidate I mentioned, he figured that out. And what a personality! Everything he says redounds to his credit. There is absolutely nothing I wouldn't do for him."

"Does Mayor Bunt know you're talking like this?" asked Melba. "Sort of zany and avaricious?"

"I'm sure he does," said Don Pond. "His spies are everywhere. I can't look for them in more than one place at a time. It's against the laws of physics. If I check under the couch, who's to guarantee they haven't darted into the corner, or run all the way into the kitchen?"

"I heard something under the couch," said Melba. "And noises were coming from that corner as well. I thought it was animals making the noises but it could have been spies."

Don Pond looked at her incredulously and Melba blinked, her cheeks mottling with a deep, irregular blush.

"Oh, you must think I'm daft," said Melba. "I hadn't realized until now . . ."

"What did you think the animals around Dan were doing if not spying?" asked Don Pond, chuckling. Generally, his modesty prevented him from indulging his sense of superiority, but this was a special occasion, ripe for merry condescension, which could be easily attributed to a spontaneous overflow of protective tenderness rather than self-congratulation, the more immodest option, and so Don Pond chuckled on, not bothering to check his glee.

"Every animal you see in Dan is one of Mayor Bunt's henchmen!" said Don Pond. "You must be the only person in Dan who didn't know that. Hadn't you noticed the way people talk in Dan? Always skirting around the most important issues, never coming to the point? It's because we can't speak freely, not with spies in every nook and cranny."

"Did Bev Hat know?" asked Melba. Don Pond's face darkened until skin and beard seemed to run together, forming an unsuggestive blot.

"There was never any Bev Hat," said Don Pond. "She was a fabrication, invented by Mayor Blunt to stir sympathies. The young mother who died tragically in the service of our glorious mayor! It's perfect isn't it?"

"If there was never any Bev Hat," Melba caught her breath as the implication struck her. "If there was never any Bev Hat, then she can't have returned from the dead as Melba Zuzzo! I knew I hadn't become Bev Hat, but I was still so disturbed . . . the very idea that I might suddenly be someone I didn't think I was before. A wife and mother at that!"

"I'm glad you're relieved," said Don Pond. "Some women would be disappointed. Bev Hat was the feminine ideal. No man was immune to her charms."

"I am glad," said Melba. Don Pond dropped the hand vacuum on the table. It clunked. Melba looked at the hand vacuum then back at Don Pond. His eyes bore into hers and he pulled a small pad out of his back pocket, making a note with a tiny pencil.

"How would you rate the gladness?" he asked. "On a scale of one to ten."

Melba began to feel uneasy.

"It's average gladness," she said. "Maybe that means I'm not glad at all? I'm just existing without actively ruing anything in particular. I suppose I'm numb rather than glad. But given how much pain there is in the world, I should think I'm glad to be numb? So maybe numbness is a form of being glad after all."

"Five?" asked Don Pond. Melba inched forward on the couch. It had grown humid in Don Pond's house and the vapors in the air pushed against her. She felt as though she was wading through a pack of damp Labradors. The dim light that came through the windows illuminated the suspended water molecules, which had grown larger, and Melba saw the graininess of the air more distinctly than the objects she hoped to see *through* the air: the room's furniture and wall-hangings, its doors. Everything around her was gray and somewhat obscured.

"At first I thought there was an obscurity inhering in my perceptions," murmured Melba. "But it's coming from the room, I'm sure of it. The room is making a cloud."

Don Pond seemed to be approaching, but she could not see him any more clearly as he neared; the graininess was growing more marked between them.

"I wonder what you'd look like without a beard?" she asked.

"Why do you wonder?" Don Pond's voice was steady.

"I don't really wonder," said Melba. "It's just sooner or later, if one person has a beard and is in the company of another person, the beard becomes a topic. I should have said something else about the beard, a statement and not a question. I should have shared a fact maybe. Did you know that growing a beard that's a different color from the rest of your hair is an expression of weakness in the genes? Oh no, that was somehow still a question, wasn't it? Well, the point is that the brain of the man with this kind of beard tends to go soft. Your beard is very uniform in color and very small and thick, and it matches your eyebrows and your head hair quite exactly, and, you know, it doesn't look quite real, not for a man, it looks like it was produced by a mink and then cut into the shape of a beard and stuck onto your face, and I was just wondering if you could take it off, oh," said Melba, flustered. "I've done it again. Leave your beard on, I don't care." She smoothed her own hair with damp palms, then smoothed her apron, then moved her shoulders up and down as she'd seen her mother do so many times, limbering.

"Well," she said, brightly. "I think I'll be going."

Don Pond raised his eyebrows, which looked very much like two wedges cut from either side of his beard, rotated 180 degrees, and stuck on above his eyes.

"Where will you go?" asked Don Pond.

"I'll go home," laughed Melba, aware that the sound of her laughter and the convulsions of her diaphragm were out of sync. One or the other was delayed. She felt vaguely nauseated by it and stopped laughing abruptly.

"Isn't that where people go?" she continued, uncertainly. "When they . . . go? If they're not already there? Home, I mean?"

She slid closer to the cushion's edge and caught her breath. The couch seemed higher. She tried to grip the black vinyl. Slowly, she stretched out her legs, straining, pointing her toes. The carpet was somewhere below, out of reach.

"You should call first," said Don Pond. He circled around the table and reached out to Melba. Don Pond's hand was cool and pale and unnaturally smooth.

"That's skin?" asked Melba, rotating her fingers in his grasp.

"Oh," said Don Pond, and tugged so that Melba's feet thudded down.

"It wasn't so far, after all," she said, straightening her knees and standing upright. "But if you're afraid of heights, it doesn't really matter how high up you are, does it? It's like how you can drown in an inch of water? My mother told me about a schoolmate of hers, Josie Pride, who drowned crying in bed. You should never cry in bed, face down obviously, but even face up or on your side, it depends on the planes of your face, how the water runs, but really, everyone's nose and mouth is downhill of the eyes, and when Josie Pride was discovered she was scarcely recognizable. Her parents thought at first she'd been abducted and some puffy dummy had been jammed under the bedclothes as a decoy, because abductions *do* happen in Dan, all the time, said my mother, and the abductors have been known to leave dummies in place of the abducted children, not as decoys, but as poppets designed to tempt the parents into pagan acts of sympathetic magic, just for fun, said my mother, because abductors in Dan are those listless types who turn to devilry to stay awake, trampling circles in people's yards, using the blood of children to raise chthonic gods of madness and corruption, and they told my mother they wanted me in particular, because my blood is tainted and tainted blood is more compelling to chthonic gods than untainted blood, and my mother had to hold them off by giving them the allowance money she would have given me otherwise and sometimes threatening violent retaliation, and if I exhausted her too much with needs and wants she would have gotten tired and stopped holding them off altogether, so I had to leave her alone and not bother her about snacks and shoes and new dresses with pretty smocking and things of that nature or she'd have let them drag me away and open up my chest on an altar that would have just been an old telephone cable spool so I'd have gotten splinters too, but don't cry about it, my mother said, or you'll drown, like Josie Pride, who wasn't a dummy after all, but was herself, wet and dead on the bottom bunk, and . . ."

Melba suspected that she was blathering. She couldn't make out what she was saying but her voice droned on and on. Don Pond was leading her by the hand, that was the reason. Melba hadn't been led by the hand in quite some time and had forgotten the loosening effect it had on the tongue.

Don Pond led her through thickening mist into a narrow corridor.

"Did you leave the tea kettle boiling?" asked Melba but Don Pond didn't answer. Melba slid the fingers of her free hand along the dark paneling that seemed to press in against her. It was damp and rough and when she hooked her fingers they bumped and snagged again and again on little dips and rises. The animal sounds were louder, coming from both sides of the corridor, and from above: chirping, rustling, mewling, rapid, wheezy breaths.

"Here's the phone," said Don Pond. It wasn't a wall phone, the kind one finds in a business, but a phone installed on a horizontal surface, in a small alcove in the wall at chest height, the kind of phone one finds in a house. Melba had never dialed her own number, but it happened to be one of the most common sequences of numerals, and she dialed confidently.

"It's ringing," she said. "Hello."

"Hello," said Mark Rand.

"Is everything quite alright?" asked Melba. "At the house?"

"You left dishes in the sink, Melba," said Mark Rand, reprovingly. Melba tucked the receiver more firmly between her ear and shoulder and hunched into the wall, hoping Don Pond couldn't hear her conversation.

"I didn't," she whispered. "One dish maybe. And my coffee mug."

"Dishes," insisted Mark Rand. "I've documented them. This isn't the first time, Melba. Have you been watering your plants on a schedule? Don't answer. You haven't been. Two of them are dead and the rest are performing poorly. There are no towels in the bathroom. Your bedroom hamper is full of unlaundered clothing."

Melba squeezed the phone receiver as hard as she could, hunching, and did not respond. She heard Mark Rand sigh.

"Melba," said Mark Rand. "You may not know this, but many landlords do not provide their tenants with washers and dryers. Tenants don't launder their clothing, say these landlords. Tenants are unkempt, disorderly people. They refuse to better themselves. I always disagree with these landlords. I provide my tenants with washers and dryers, I say. I give my tenants the opportunity to launder their clothing. I don't want to see my tenants licking their coats on the street, I say. My tenants are men and women of quality. My tenants smell fresh, I say. It's a pleasure to stand close to my tenants. Touching my tenants poses no significant risk."

"I was planning on laundering my clothing just as soon as I could," said Melba. "I'll do it right now. I'm on my way home and I'll launder at once."

"No!" Mark Rand's voice was hard. "I don't want your explanations and promises, and if I did I would want them in writing. Sometimes I think the telephone was invented by a jealous manufacturer with an anti-landlord agenda as an instrument of torture. Manufacturers loathe landlords! Do you know why? Because landlords defy the mercantile system! Instead of obeying the dictates of the market and pursuing their self-interest, landlords selflessly pursue the interests of their tenants! I am speaking of true landlords, naturally, those who dedicate themselves to the broad human purpose of providing their fellow men and women with the benefits of roofs and walls, and in special cases, windows, doors, indoor plumbing, electric lights, etc., etc., and in the rarest cases, washers and dryers, dishes and cutlery, house plants, and precious antiques. True landlords expect to find enemies among the merchants, but it is more than the true landlord can bear when a tenant comes under the sway of manufacturers, plays into a manufacturer's hands, uses the telephone provided by the manufacturers to plague and harry the landlord just as the manufacturers intended! Tenants should side with the landlord *against* the manufacturer, but tenants rarely act in their own best interests, which is precisely why they need landlords to begin with."

"I know I need you!" Melba cried. "I've never even met a manufacturer, at least not that I know of. Don't they wear tall hats? I'm sure I wouldn't side with a person like that. I wouldn't have called at all but Don Pond suggested it, I think as a formality, because it's always polite to call home, not so as to plague or harry you!"

"Don Pond," said Mark Rand. "Why are you taking suggestions from Don Pond?"

"I'm a guest in his house," said Melba. She glanced over her shoulder at Don Pond who stood in the attitude of a man who was not overhearing a nearby telephone conversation but was rather immersing himself in his own thoughts, thoughts that were thoroughly amusing. His head was tilted to one side and he was looking up toward the ceiling, smiling steadily through his beard. "When the landlord is not present, shouldn't the guest take suggestions from the landlord's tenant? Isn't that the chain of command?"

"And how do you know that the landlord is not present?" asked Mark Rand. "Is Don Pond's house so small and devoid of mystery that you can be certain the landlord does not lurk undetected, perhaps in order to test you, and in so testing you, test *me*, to ascertain what kind of tenant I produce? Taking Don Pond's suggestions, Melba, you are no doubt failing a test on my behalf. The only way to distance myself from this failure would be to terminate your tenancy."

"Leslie Duck is Don Pond's landlord!" said Melba. "Leslie Duck is not present. He left Dan to buy a banana plantation. He must be a thousand miles away, on an island, maybe on the exact island I drew as a little girl. I have no idea where that island is but it was the farthest thing I could imagine from Dan at the time I drew it. I didn't know anything about the moon back then, or the wormholes that lead you through the galaxy into something entirely unknown and maybe nonexistent, that is, according to the instruments we use to determine if something exists. I'm sure the other side of wormholes exists for the creatures that live there. Leslie Duck probably isn't as far from Dan as that, who knows if bananas grow on the other sides of wormholes, but he's nowhere nearby."

"Who told you that, Melba?" asked Mark Rand. "Think carefully. Who told you that Leslie Duck was far away, farming bananas?"

"Officer Greg," whispered Melba at the same time that Mark Rand cried out "Officer Greg!" in a tone of exultation.

"That's right!" said Mark Rand. "Officer Greg, who, as you well know, sleeps on a cot in the Dan Police Station. Who do you think owns the Dan Police Station?"

Melba hesitated.

"Leslie Duck!" said Mark Rand. "Officer Greg is Leslie Duck's tenant. Officer Greg and Don Pond haven't failed their landlord the way you've failed me, Melba. Leslie Duck is enjoying my defeat, let me tell you, and not from afar. From right around the corner!"

Melba clutched the receiver to her chest and looked up and down the corridor. She could see nothing Leslie Duck-like in the murky distance, but the murky distance might conceal any number of corners around which Leslie Duck crouched, enjoying Mark Rand's defeat to the utmost, which was a word that made Melba pause.

Utmost.

Had she heard Principal Benjamin discussing a planet Utmost with the astronaut in those few seconds she'd hovered above the desk in the cafeteria, before the hand closed upon her neck and yanked her back?

"Melba, I have no choice," said Mark Rand. "I can't be your landlord under these circumstances. It wouldn't be in your best interests to have a failure for a landlord. Consider yourself evicted. Your possessions revert to me in lieu of my collecting monies against damages to the property. Do you own anything of particular value?"

"No," said Melba, slowly.

"Once again you've gotten the long end of the stick, Melba," said Mark Rand. "Someday you may accumulate enough of those sticks to build yourself a shelter, and then you'll be done with landlords altogether. Until then may every clemency attend your slumbers in the open fields of Dan."

Melba returned the receiver softly to its cradle. Don Pond started, as though until hearing that click, he'd been so absorbed in his reflections he'd quite forgotten that Melba had been engaged in a heated telephone conversation mere inches to his left. He blinked at the telephone.

"Nice phone call?" he asked.

"Nice enough," said Melba. "I can't go home though." She spread out her arms, palms slightly upraised. The gesture expressed a sentiment similar to that expressed by a shrug. It expressed the same sentiment, but amplified to a power of 1.5.

"I have nowhere to go," said Melba.

"It's a problem in small towns," said Don Pond, sympathetically. "The only way to leave is to go nowhere. But that takes a certain type of resolve."

"Like Principal Benjamin," said Melba. "He didn't go anywhere anyone knows of, and so he's just gone."

"You can't get over him, can you?" asked Don Pond, sadly. "He's always been there between us. In a way, he's the least gone man in Dan. He looms larger than life every time I meet your eyes."

Melba slid her eyes as quickly as she could from the vicinity of Don Pond's. She was unemployed and homeless and had failed who knows how many tests. She could not now meet the eyes of a man who moped and spoke of looming.

"Let's not meet eyes," said Melba. "I'm too grim and I wouldn't want to curse you inadvertently. Don't lead me by the hand either. If you start walking I can follow you easily enough. The terrain isn't rough."

"Fine," said Don Pond curtly.

"The floor slopes," he said over his shoulder, continuing down the corridor.

Melba murmured something indistinct and assenting. They entered a small kitchen. A man was standing at the kitchen stove stirring a large pot. He turned when they entered. The man's coloring was not particularly dark but he gave the impression of darkness, most likely due to his crowded features, and the long, dark, well-tailored coat he wore even though kitchen work is not cooling. Melba felt that the heat stifled, but the man breathed lightly and his skin bore no sheen. The kitchen smelled powerfully of vinegar and damp grains.

"Dinner is a surprise," said the man, holding out his wooden spoon to prevent their approach.

Don Pond nodded his small head vigorously.

"We're passing through, Helmut," he said. "We absolutely will not peer." To Melba he said in a loud whisper: "It's always entertaining to pass by a European. They take offense at the least thing and want to duel you with swords or pistols or else they burst into storming sobs or give you ominous counsel and if they're feeling expansive they present you with oddments from a storied cigar box of oddments which they claim to have taken with them on many journeys by boat."

"What kind of oddments?" whispered Melba dutifully.

"Sheep vertebra, digestive biscuits, potsherds, triangular coins," said Don Pond, waving his hand vaguely to indicate "and so on" or "things of that nature."

"Ah," said Melba. The man had returned his attention to the pot on the stove.

"He's really from another country?" asked Melba.

"That's what we assume," said Don Pond. "Dan has its home-grown Europeans to be sure, but Helmut Pirm doesn't mix with them. He says they speak gibberish and if you allow them to take your coat they fill the pockets with mothballs."

"I've seen his mansard," said Melba. "Does he make good dinners?"

"He makes surprising dinners," said Don Pond. "Watch me sidle to that door then do the same." Don Pond sidled to the door. Helmut Pirm stirred his pot. Melba tried not to investigate Helmut Pirm or his vicinity as she sidled after Don Pond but she noticed that he had lined up a row of spices and a bird on the counter.

She stopped behind Don Pond who had stopped before the door. The door opened inward and Don Pond stepped back and sideways, as though he too were a door, a door that opened outward. He gestured Melba through the door and she went through it, feeling uncomfortably aware that she had passed through the Don Pond door to reach the kitchen door—the second door, Melba said to herself.

The room she had entered was narrow, no windows, walls of recessed shelves bearing boxes, bottles, sacks, and jars of foodstuffs rising to the low ceiling. Across from the door, at the other end of the room, there was a wooden ladder. Don Pond was crowding her forward so that he could shut the kitchen door, the second door, behind them. The room was so small that Melba was soon pressed against the ladder. She put her foot on the first rung. From the second rung, she could press up on the hatch in the ceiling. She pressed up and began to climb through the hatch. Her head and shoulders emerged into the amber air of the upper story, and she saw the pant legs of many men. Tilting her head, she saw entire men, ranged all about.

"I'm terribly sorry," she said. A few of the men glanced over but most took no notice. A fair number of them were grouped together with their backs to the hatch, studying a wall. Melba squinted. There was an image on the wall, dots and lines either drawn across its dull surface or drawn upon a large sheet of wheat-pasted paper, but as Melba peered, ascending a rung on the ladder and craning her neck to get a better vantage from her position, halfway out of the hatch, she realized the dots and lines were not drawn at all. They were dimensional. She saw that there were pins in the wall, dozens of pins, some long, protruding far from the wall's surface, shanks stacked with beads, others short, more like tacks, their wider, flattened tops covered in plaid cloth. Colored strings stretched from pin to pin, although some of the strings might well have been wire, Melba thought, heated piano wire, or perhaps fishing line, so often purposed for other things, Zeno Zuzzo had once explained, coiling the line from wrist to wrist, such as the looping of a garrote, and the pins and strings created a vast web, with, it seemed, infinite hubs, radii, spirals, and frames, and Melba fixed her gaze, straining to look through the wall, wondering if a picture might resolve in the foreground, rising out of the hopelessly irregular design. Her eyes watered and she blinked. Her eyes felt spent, limp, and the water continued to drip from the incontinent ducts.

Suddenly, a man broke from the group. He stepped closer to the wall, pressed the point of a black pin against it, and sank the shank deeply with three practiced blows of a lozenge-shaped eraser. He stepped back and another man sprang to take his place, wrapping the end of the pin again and again with gold embroidery floss. Melba watched, curious as to what the man would do with the other end of the floss: attach it to another pin presumably, but which?

She felt a knocking on her calves. Don Pond wanted to ascend the ladder and Melba remained half in and half out, stalled between rooms. She tried to whisper down the hatch, "I believe it's some kind of club, Don. A private men's club. I'm not a member. I don't think I should . . ." but the knocking on her calves sped up and began to sting, even through her skirts. Sighing, Melba struggled through the hatch, bracing herself with her arms then dragging up her knees.

A moment later Don Pond shot up through the hatch. Melba hung back as Don Pond circulated. She stood, fidgeting, a few paces from the open hatch and its lid, a hinged square of raw wood. She stepped forward once to toe the lid over, intending to close the hatch and reseal the space, feeling guiltily as though, by leaving the hatch open, she was allowing a kind of leak to persist, a leak which might eventually deflate the private men's club altogether, so that the room and everything in it shriveled. She lifted the lid an inch with her toe then reconsidered. Was it better not to meddle? She stepped back, trying to detect in the room and in the men any sign that in fact the club was leaking, looking about for increasing flaccidity, listening for a high whine.

The hatch had not opened into the middle of the room. It had opened into the middle of the bottom right square of the room, if the room could be thought of as a four-square court, with the men studying the wall occupying the top left square. Melba suspected that the kitchen was beneath the bottom left square of the room. She sniffed and smelled no vinegar. The air was dry and tangy. Everywhere she looked there were men: men pacing, men standing, men sitting, men crouching, men lying on their backs, men lying on their stomachs, men lying on their sides. Melba swallowed, hesitant to seem as though she studied these men. She cast about for objects upon which to drop her gaze. Everyone knew that men in private men's clubs preferred to protect their identities.

And here was Melba Zuzzo, thought Melba Zuzzo, self-accusation and self-pity warring within her, here she was, standing uninvited in the middle of one quarter of a private men's club, identifying men left and right! She tried to blot out the names before they registered in her mind, but she realized she was moving her lips, shaping the names with her mouth. Bert Bus. Hal Drake. Grady Help. Seton Holmes. She clapped a hand over her mouth. She would never have put herself in this position intentionally.

Damn Don Pond, she thought.

"This must be a faux-pas!" she burst out. "And it's your fault Don Pond!"

The men nearest by, those standing in a line that described the top of Melba's square, brushing the shoulders of each other's sports jackets with tiny brushes, all turned their heads to look in her direction. Don Pond, charging over from the top right square, pushed through the line of men and marched right up to Melba, who sagged at his approach.

"Oh, now I've done it," she said miserably. "I've identified you. I shouted 'Don Pond!' for all to hear, and you probably use a different name in this context, like Shorty or Fats Fish. I'm no good up here. I'll wreck everything. I don't know why you brought me."

Melba's nose burned and she dug her nails into her palms. She realized that, in her sagging, she had allowed her neck to wilt and her head hung lower than she'd thought possible. It hung heavily and her neck offered no resistance. Her head swung slightly as it sank and sank. The carpet filled her field of vision. It was a dull carpet, institutional beige, designed for moderate to heavy traffic, new or recently cleaned, nylon, no off-gas, utterly inert. Melba felt as though she were executing the slowest swan dive in the world. She was diving into the carpet. She had penetrated deep inside the carpet. The fibers twisted around her this way and that. She had come too close; she could no longer see the pattern of the weave. Its curves formed the dimensional space in which she bobbed, weightless.

Matter has but one pattern, thought Melba, rotating, seeing the fibers branch and branch again, those branches branching off, the shapes they composed creating a whole that was the same shape as every part.

The subdivisions are infinite, thought Melba. Infinite and identical. The distributions of fibers in the carpet, of cells in her body, of bodies in the room, of rooms in the house, and of houses in Dan—they were indistinguishable, each from the others. At a certain range, Dan wasn't any different from the mountains that surrounded it or from the craters on the moon. Maybe, without difference to separate one thing from the other, distances vanished. She could be anywhere, with anyone. She could walk around inside herself and there would be sacks of dark apples, culverts, sudden rises and muddy declivities, swamps and meres and woods and rotted leaves to nestle into, mosses that would sing her to sleep. She could continue sinking, headfirst, diving slowly down onto the carpet. She could roll onto her back on the carpet. She could lie quietly.

"Maybe I'm over-tired," she murmured, stiffening her neck, striving to right herself. Turgor pressure? Was that what she needed?

"I wonder if all these men drink tea or if there's coffee . . ."

"Coffee's in the kitchen, Melba," said Don Pond. He had reached her side. No longer charging, he no longer seemed bullish. He didn't look in the least likely to stamp and snort and toss her broken body high in the air. He displayed the chumminess of a man enjoying himself in the midst of men and seemed untroubled by Melba's rash, nominating shout. His chumminess only deepened as he addressed her. "Poor Melba! You missed your chance. Europeans make small coffee so I'm not surprised you didn't see it!" He laughed. "The coffee was right there. You walked right past it."

Melba tried to smile.

"I know I was accusing just now," she said. "I felt gawky and out of place, but not anymore. This is a wonderful club, Don."

"Wonderful? I don't know about that," said Don Pond. "But men have to congregate somewhere. We wouldn't be men if we were dispersed, if we were each of us all by himself. Do you recognize those potted plants? Or those magazines?"

"It's been a long time," said Melba. "But the whole place, the men, plants, magazines, chairs, carpet, overhead lights, it does seem familiar. It reminds me of Dr. Buck's waiting room."

"A long time you say? Doesn't it always feel like a long time in waiting rooms!" Don Pond's enjoyment was only increasing. He rubbed his pale hands together and they squeaked.

"Is Randal Hans here?" Melba allowed herself to scan the men in the bottom left square of the room, the men who sat in broad low chairs, leafing through magazines, or using shoe horns to remove their boots, settling in to wait with stocking feet. She doubted Randal Hans would be among the more vigorous men, the men clustered at the wall with their pins and spools and packets, using tiny rulers to measure angles, consulting pocket notebooks then pointing at some pin from which several dozen strings radiated, crying out in protest, but neither did she see him among the men seated in chairs. She looked over the heads of these seated men, looked intently at those men sticking and wrapping and crying out at the wall. Suddenly Ned Hat spun away from the wall and glared at her, his mouth bristling with pins.

"A bald cap," supplied Don Pond, guessing the source of Melba's confusion. "This morning. He was wearing a rubber bald cap."

Melba nodded. Ned Hat's hair did not brush his shoulders, but it curved away from his scalp in a globe the bottom curves of which turned inward to brush, on either side, against his jaw. She would have been hard-pressed to believe he could have managed to grow such hair since she'd seen him last, although it seemed ages since she'd stared up at the bald, frothing man in the window.

Of course, time moves differently when considered from the point of view of hair. Time is slower for hair and yields to a progress narrative—the hair extruding in lengthening shafts—until each hair reaches its maximum length and progress stops. But what about curly hair? Hair that coils around and around? Melba strained, thinking. If she could consider time from the perspective of her hair, which was dead, a waste material, but which would continue to lengthen after she herself was dead . . .

Think, she whispered, think, think.

"He's wearing a rubber mask too," said Don Pond. Melba let her fingers drop from her temples where she had pressed them, turning them rapidly back and forth, like drill bits skipping in stripped screws.

No good, the thinking. She observed Ned Hat.

"A rubber mask? I wouldn't have been able to tell," she said.

"No?" said Don Pond. "It's a rubber mask of Ned Hat's face. Can't you tell that's Ned Hat?"

Melba paused. Ned Hat spat the pins in her direction. His tongue emerged to prod his lips then retracted. He whipped a pocket notebook from inside his sports coat and spun back to face the wall, pointing, crying out in protest.

"Yes?" said Melba. "But what about Randal Hans?"

"Randal Hans," Don Pond thought for moment. "The notary public? Chin dimple, left shoulder higher than the right? The one running for mayor? Randal Hans! His platform is based on selling Dan for fill, which isn't anything on which to base a platform!"

"I don't understand," blinked Melba.

"Backhoes, Melba. Dumptrucks. Dig into Dan as far we can go and ship out the soil. People pay top dollar for dirt."

"What people?" asked Melba.

"Coastal people," said Don Pond. "People afraid of the surging seas. Valley people. People tired of the imperious gazes of hilltop neighbors. Desert people. People who want to plant hyacinths. People! I don't know which people in particular. A good number of sextons, I imagine. Their bread-and-butter depends on burial plots keeping pace with the booming population. But no one will vote for Randal Hans if he's propounding such an idea! Not because there isn't a demand for dirt. There is! Because what is Dan without the dirt it is built on?"

"A void, I suppose?" said Melba. Don Pond was leaning closer, his face approaching Melba's. His moist eyes gleamed from deep within thick folds, black eyebrows suspended over them.

"The abyss," he said hoarsely. "Everything we do, frantic activities, assignations of meaning to random gestures and grunts, succorings of our organisms and the organisms of those to whom we've developed attachments—it's all designed to distract us from the very abyss in which we formed, the formlessness that fills us. Melba, the infinite emptying of everything . . . this is the only process! It doesn't matter if it's reversed. It is changeless! Do you see why Randal Hans can't win? He comes too close to the horror. He scrapes against it with his plan, scooping Dan away by the shovelful. He's a figure of horror as well, the jutting chin, nearly cloven, the twisted shoulders, the shrunken legs. He only comes up to my waist. His legs are so weak they often collapse, folding beneath him at grotesque angles, and he pulls himself through Dan with his arms, creeping through the gutters, singing a little song, a haunting little song. You've heard it. It comes from those gutters and from beneath the bed. It comes from within the twisted channels of our ears. It's so soft. It's so high and thin. It never stops. I hear it even now . . ." Don Pond drew a breath as though preparing to sing, or scream.

"Stop!" cried Melba. "Stop, stop! I don't think we're talking about the same Randal Hans at all."

Don Pond's smile returned. "Of course we are. It's all the same Randal Hans. Let me show you something." He reached out to grasp her hand. Melba rapidly clasped her hands behind her back.

"This is the classical way to walk," she said. "The Attic manner. We're in an attic, aren't we?" She tittered nervously. "I do believe in the civic benefits of a classical education, I'm not abashed to admit it anymore. Don't you? Principal Benjamin used to have us all recite the Hippocratic Oath at morning assembly."

"He did, did he? Principal Benjamin?" Don Pond's inscrutability impressed her. It was perfect. Perfect inscrutability. Melba remembered that some things are always useless to scrutinize, maybe most things, maybe everything. Behind her back she wrung her clasped hands.

"Follow me," said Don Pond. He walked past Melba toward the corner of the room, the bottom right corner in Melba's square of the room. Melba turned. Don Pond was waiting for her in front of a door. The door had a dark stain and a small brass plate with faint engraving.

"Hurry," he said. "Don't let the men see." He turned the knob and the door swung inward. Don Pond swung away from the door, toward Melba who stood poised on her toes, undecided and perturbed. She didn't want to follow Don Pond, but she didn't want him to disappear through a door, either, leaving her with the men.

"Go on," he urged, and Melba walked up to him, almost shuffling, dragging her feet. Her stout, supportive shoes seemed heavier than usual. She opened her mouth.

"Go on!" Don Pond pivoted and suddenly he was behind her, herding her forward. Melba drew in her breath. She lurched across the threshold. The door clicked as Don Pond pulled it shut. Don Pond and Melba Zuzzo stood side by side on fresh green linoleum.

"I thought for sure there'd be someone in here!" said Melba, relieved.

"You're relieved," observed Don Pond.

"I've been in offices before," said Melba, stung by the note of reproach. "More offices than you might think. I wouldn't mind encountering a person in his office. I know the protocols!" She glanced at Don Pond who was watching her closely. She looked away.

"It's just that, usually, when I went to an office, I had an appointment," she explained, "or if not an appointment, a purpose in visiting, a question to ask or a disciplinary measure to fulfill. That makes it easier, in the beginning of the visit at least, when you're warming up. You don't have to work as hard to explain yourself." She risked another glance at Don Pond. He stood so close beside her that the smallest rotation of her head brought their faces into shocking proximity. His eyes still shone, gaze fixed upon her. She inched her body to the left, rotating her head carefully back to center.

"The rules might have changed," she admitted, inching yet farther. "I haven't been to an office since I was a girl. This looks like a doctor's office, but if it were a doctor's office wouldn't I have had to sign something? A consent form? Or is it different now? Maybe if you consented once, no matter how long ago, that's enough." She caught sight of the framed picture on the wall and started.

"I drew that!" she said.

"Why, so you did," said Don Pond. Forgetting herself, Melba rushed to the wall. The wall was smooth, windowless, painted green, a far paler shade than the linoleum, with an eggshell finish. The drawing was the only decoration. Melba touched her forefinger to the thin gold frame. She stared at the drawing behind the layer of glass.

"But it isn't any good," laughed Melba. "It was the worst picture in the whole class! Mrs. Page didn't put in the display case with the others."

"Maybe that's because someone else took an interest in it and put it somewhere else," suggested Don Pond. Melba squinted at the picture and tried to imagine someone taking an interest in it. She couldn't. It was too difficult to imagine. She shook her head.

"I can't even tell what it's supposed to be," said Melba. "The as-

Dan

signment was to draw a picture of your family, but that's not my family. It's only one figure, but with too many limbs, or maybe it's a figure holding an animal? Joe Moore sat next to me in drawing class and he ate the colored crayons, that's why it's all black and white and gray. This doesn't belong on an office wall! Even an office with no secretary outside and nobody in it."

"We're in the office, aren't we, Melba?" asked Don Pond. He dropped into a rolling chair and pulled the chair forward with his legs until he was just in front of the drawing, gazing up at it. Melba had to step aside to make room for him. She moved over into the corner and her elbow touched something cold, the metal basin of a sink.

"It's my favorite drawing," said Don Pond. "Do you want to wash your elbow?"

"Oh no, thank you," said Melba hurriedly, folding up her arms and touching both elbows together in front of her, hands clasped. It wasn't the most comfortable attitude she had ever assumed. Don Pond's keen gaze missed nothing.

"You're not comfortable," he said. "It's important to make yourself comfortable. Lie down," said Don Pond.

"Would that be alright?" said Melba. "Sometimes lying down when you're not absolutely by yourself can be construed as rude, or presumptuous, or just strange! I can stand here. It's very pleasant. What a nice sink." She realized she was grinding her elbows together. Don Pond rolled slowly toward her.

"I do like lying down, though," said Melba. "Particularly on top of tables. I like sitting under tables too, but you couldn't sit under this one." She didn't turn her back on Don Pond. Instead she sidled along the wall then darted into the middle of the room. She hoisted herself onto the narrow table and lay back. She crossed her arms behind her head. Her neck felt stiff, tipped up. Her hands introduced too much space between her occiput and shoulders. She had the uneasy feeling that her head might pop free. She put her arms at her sides. She wiggled and the paper that covered the table's layer of thin, hard cushioning crinkled.

"The paper on this table is just like the paper I used for my drawing," Melba murmured. "Mrs. Page had rolls of it in the closet. I could have made my drawing much longer. I could have taken the roll and found someone to turn it, Joe Moore even, and I could have kept drawing as he turned, drawn on and on. Then we'd have the whole drawing instead of just a square of it. You can't tell much from just a square of something. I'm sure there should have been more to this drawing, on either side of it. There's always more on either side of something. Except maybe it's always more of the same thing, and the tiniest square tells you everything . . ." Even with her hands at her side, Melba felt that the space between occiput and shoulders was getting larger. Soon her head would be floating. Her thoughts came from farther and farther away.

"You don't need more than a single moment to understand time, do you?" She wasn't sure whom she was addressing. The question wasn't for Don Pond. The question hovered, like her head, detached from everything. She pushed more air through her lips, struggling to form the words.

"I tried to think about time all at once, was that my problem?" Her voice was a whisper. "Was that what I was always doing wrong, over and over again, every moment?" Melba's next words slurred and dispersed. She couldn't make them out. She heard a hissing. It didn't come from her, or from animals. It was a different kind of hissing, a sound shallower and more sustained: the sound of gas escaping from a valve. She tried to detect an odor, the odor of the gas, but the gas was odorless. The room was filled with an odorless gas; it had to be. There was no odor in the room and the hissing did not stop. The hissing continued. Melba blinked against the strong light that beamed from directly above.

"I can't see the drawing at all from here," she said. She shut her eyes. She heard the chair rolling toward her, the clunk of the trucks striking the bottom of the table. Her face felt hot and the darkness behind her closed eyelids bloomed red, the redness widening, yellow corollas pushing out from the centers. She knew the light source had been swung closer and she jerked, almost rising, but her fear of the burning bulb restrained her. She gripped the padded edges of the table.

Gripping is good, thought Melba. Gripping is always good. Come what may, it helps to find an edge, a dowel, a hem. It helps to hold it, hold on to it tightly. Even if you are lying quietly, on your back, waiting for everything to pass, you still need to grasp something, with your teeth if you don't have hands, and if you don't have teeth, with your gums, and if you don't have gums . . .

Melba moved her jaws, felt her teeth work together, uppers against the lowers.

If you don't have teeth, she thought, if you don't have gums, if you don't have jaws, if the top of your skull is lifting . . .

"You can't see the drawing?" The voice came from close above, a soft, stroking voice, emanating from the heat and the light, merging with her burning face, forming part of its lid of blooming red.

I can't speak, thought Melba. I'm already speaking. That explains it. A person can't speak if she's already speaking.

"You can't see?" said the voice. "You can't see?"

I will be remembered, thought Melba, if I am remembered, as someone of whom too much was asked. Provided of course, thought Melba, that I am the one remembering. But will that ever be certain? That I am the one? The one Melba Zuzzo? Melba. Melba Zuzzo. Melba? Melba Zuzzo? You can't see? Are you sure? Can you be sure? You can't see the man in the drawing? You can't see Benjamin? He's standing right there, against the wall. He is dressed in gray. You can see him, a gray figure. Behind him: a black wall. The wall encloses the town. You can't see the town, but you can see the man and the wall.

He's outside then, thought Melba. Outside the town. And so I am, if that's what I see, if that's what I drew. I'm outside. Was I always?

The light hurt. She covered her eyes with her palms.

She felt a crinkle beneath her, like a ripple of water, but of course not like a ripple of water. The crinkle was dry. The paper layer that covered the table was rolling beneath her, rolling and rolling, and she lay unmoving above it.

"Oh!" Melba cried. "Oh." The friction filled her with shocks. She felt a twinge of pain. The movement of the paper heated her scalp, roughed and tangled her hairs.

"You can stop turning the roll," said Melba. "I don't need nearly this much."

But beneath her the paper rolled on.

"Far away," said Melba, "on another landmass, there's a curious river. It has a long, wide meander with carbon black banks that dye the water for miles. It's a river of ink. Does that ring a bell?"

She had been told of this river, by someone, she couldn't think who, a pen dealer whose regional aircraft had dropped out of the sky over Dan, crashing almost gently into the swamp.

This river moving under her body—it was a river of paper, not a river of ink. Paper and ink. They were opposites, really. Or on the diagonal, kitty-corner. And what trumped what? A river of paper or a river of ink?

"I used to play a game with my father," said Melba, "where one hand trumped another. He always shouted to break my concentration. Or he made shapes with his hand that beat everything, mostly bombs or flesh-eating bacteria. I never won a single time."

She imagined hands all around her, hands encased in latex, pale green and pale blue, hands making unbeatable shapes, bombs and comets and tsunamis and super-volcanoes and the heat-death of the universe.

The room is filling with hands, she thought. There are slots in the walls and in the floor and in the ceiling and the men are poking their hands into the room.

She felt something small and cold press down on her chest.

"Don," she said. "Is that you? Who's there?"

Above the hissing, she heard a new sound, a faltering melody, half hummed, half whispered. It was a horrible, haunting little song. She held her breath, listening, but the song didn't have any words. She felt something cold press into her ear. She concentrated on the paper sliding beneath her, the incessant soft abrasions and electric tingles along her scalp.

"I wish I could levitate," she said. "Even if it were only with magnets and not truly magical. Would you rather fly or be invisible? Would you rather die, live forever, or never have been born? Or something else? Evaporate? You'd disappear slowly with a sure return?"

She felt a tiny sharp blow on her knee.

She felt a tiny sharp blow on her elbow.

There's a rate at which I'm vanishing, she thought. I don't think I'm someone who goes in an instant.

"I'm not getting up," she said. "Not for awhile."

Dan

The song was already fading. Something prodded her leg, very lightly, her abdomen, her neck, or it might have been an itch produced by her own skin, traveling across her body's surfaces. Below the surfaces, there were deeper layers to which the itch could not penetrate. The surface sensation traveled, dissipated.

There's a rate, she thought. But it's not the kind of thing you can calculate.

How relieved people would be. If only she could tell them.

She felt the paper moving beneath her, and she lay very still on top of it, not saying anything, not moving at all.

ABOUT THE AUTHOR

Joanna Ruocco is the author of *Another Governess/The Least Black-smith: A Diptych* (FC2, 2012), *A Compendium of Domestic Incidents* (Noemi Press, 2011), *Man's Companions* (Tarpaulin Sky Press, 2010), and *The Mothering Coven* (Ellipsis Press, 2009). A recipient of the Pushcart Prize, and winner of the Catherine Doctorow Innovative Fiction Prize, she co-edits *Birkensnake,* a fiction journal, with Brian Conn.

DOROTHY, A PUBLISHING PROJECT